"Chance,"
dropping
own. "Con

He leaned toward her, feeling drawn into her as he inhaled the warm scent of her perfume. "Help you what?"

Her reaction made him weak. That attraction—an *awareness*—pulsed between them. It was hard to resist. Passion. Chemistry. Electricity.

"Fight this," she implored, her eyes soft and filling with heat.

"Nah," he drawled slowly as he lowered his head and pressed a soft kiss to the corner of her mouth.

"Chance," she sighed, with just a hint of aching in her tone.

He shook his head as he smiled and then pressed his lips against hers.

The tip of her tongue darted out to lick at his bottom lip.

He groaned in hot pleasure, feeling his entire body jolt with an unseen surge of current. This energy created by a connection between them had been stoked for the last two weeks. Taunting and tempting them with a power that could not be ignored.

Th   n his
lif

Dear Reader,

We return to Passion Grove for the next installment in the series, *Tempting the Billionaire*. This time, the relationship of Ngozi and Chance is the focus and I am so excited for you all to enjoy their love story. It's funny that I'm the author and I was rooting for them even as I wrote the book because of their backstories. I hope you feel just as connected to them as I do.

I am truly enjoying this series. The wealth of the characters opens up so many possibilities for romance in exotic locales. The research on ultra-wealthy living was inspiring! Still, Passion Grove is the spot where they fall in love—what better place than a fictional small town centered around a heart-shaped lake with every street named after beautiful flowers?

Best,

Niobia

TEMPTING *the* BILLIONAIRE

Niobia Bryant

H HARLEQUIN® KIMANI™ ROMANCE

Recycling programs
for this product may
not exist in your area.

ISBN-13: 978-1-335-21689-2

Tempting the Billionaire

For questions and comments about the quality of this book please contact us at CustomerService@Harlequin.com.

HARLEQUIN®
www.Harlequin.com

Printed in U.S.A.

Niobia Bryant is the award-winning and national bestselling author of more than thirty works of romance and commercial mainstream fiction. Twice she has won the RT Reviewers' Choice Best Book Award for African American/Multicultural Romance. Her most recent book written under the pseudonym of Meesha Mink was listed as one of *Library Journal's* Best Books of 2014 in the African American fiction category. Her books have appeared in *Ebony*, *Essence*, the *New York Post*, the *Star-Ledger*, the *Dallas Morning News* and many other national publications. Her bestselling book, *Message from a Mistress*, was adapted to film.

"I am a writer, born and bred. I can't even fathom what else I would do besides creating stories and telling tales. When it comes to my writing I dabble in many genres, my ideas are unlimited and the ink in my pen is infinite." —Niobia Bryant

For more on this author, please visit www.niobiabryant.com.

Books by Niobia Bryant

Harlequin Kimani Romance

A Billionaire Affair
Tempting the Billionaire

Visit the Author Profile page
at Harlequin.com for more titles.

As always, for my mama/my guardian angel,
Letha "Bird" Bryant

Chapter 1

September 2018
Cabrera, Dominican Republic

Thud-thud-thud-thud-thud-thud.

Chance Castillo heard the pounding of his sneak-ered feet beating against the packed dirt as he ran up the tree-lined path breaking through the dense trees and royal palms. He made his way up the mountains that appeared green and lush against the blue skies when viewed from a distance. He didn't break his pace until he reached the top. His lean but strong muscular frame was drenched in sweat, and his heart pounded intensely in that way after great exertion—which for him was sex or running.

I've had way more of the latter lately.

He pulled his hand towel from the rim of his basketball shorts and wiped the sweat from his face and neck as he sat atop a large moss-covered rock, propping his elbows on his knees. As his pulse began to slowly decelerate, Chance looked around at his tranquil surroundings. He was surrounded by shades of green, from vibrant emerald to the muted tones of sage and olive. The smell of earth and nature was thick. He inhaled deeply, knowing he would miss his morning run from his secluded villa down along the white sand beach of the shoreline of the Atlantic Ocean to the surrounding mountains and cliff side.

His mother, Esmerelda Diaz, had transplanted her love of her beautiful hometown of Cabrera to him. As a kid, he had loved her stories of growing up on a small farm in the hills overlooking the coast in the northern region of the Dominican Republic. Her family members were hardworking farmers of fruits and vegetables whose livelihood depended on their crops. She spoke of days more bad than good. Plenty of struggle. Sometimes just a small meal away from hunger. Money spent on nothing more than bare necessities. Her life was filled with more coastal tranquility than wealth, but her memories were of a small family working hard in humble surroundings and enjoying the simple life they led.

Chance squinted his deep-set chestnut-brown eyes as he looked around at the higher elevation of the small town that was ripe with hills, oceanfront cliffs and mountains as green as emeralds. Fortunately, the town had not yet been overtaken by traffic and congestion like neighboring tourist traps. Still, there were a good number of people from other countries living in the town, experiencing the vivid Latino culture and enjoying the excellent exchange rate of American dollars while retaining their citizenship to their home country.

Chance chuckled. *Technically,* I *am an expat.*

He was a United States citizen, and although he had been living in Cabrera for the last eight months, he had every intention of returning to the States. *Back to my life.*

His brows deepened as he frowned a bit and turned his head to look off in the distance. The sun was setting, and he could just make out the outline of his sprawling two-story beachfront villa. It was the epitome of luxury living, with its private beach and sweeping views of the surrounding mountain ranges, tranquil waters, and azure skies.

It was the best his money could buy.

And seeing the smile on his mother's face when he purchased it two years prior had been worth every cent. Never had he seen her so proud. It was everything she worked for as an Afro-Dominican single mother with a broken heart and a low-paying job as a nursing assistant who was determined her son not get lost in the shuffle of the tough streets of the Soundview section of the Bronx, New York.

He still shook his head in wonder at the sacrifices the petite beauty had made for him to have a better life. Chance was ten when Esmerelda began working double shifts as a certified nursing assistant to move them out of their apartment in the Soundview projects to a better neighborhood. It meant taking on higher rent and a longer commute to her job, but she felt it was worth the sacrifice to be closer to the fringes of the Upper East Side because she wanted him to attend the elite Manhattan private academy The Dalton School. Although she applied for scholarships, she fought hard to pay his annual tuition and fees while keeping them clothed, fed and with a roof over their heads.

Chance's heart swelled with love for his mother. He'd never forgotten or taken her sacrifice for granted. It motivated him. Her happiness was his fuel through the tough days adjusting to being the poor kid who felt different from his classmates. He went on to finish at Dalton and graduated from Harvard with a degree in accounting and finance. While making a good living in finance, six years later he became a self-made wealthy man in his own right after selling a project management app for well over $600 million. That, plus the dividends from smart investing, was rocketing him toward billionaire status. He had purchased a home in Alpine, New Jersey, for his mother and ordered her retirement—she gladly agreed.

That was three years ago.

I'm not the poor kid from the Bronx with the two uniforms and the cheap shoes anymore.

In the distance, Chance heard the up-tempo beat of Ozuna and Cardi B's "La Modelo." He looked back over his shoulder, and at the top of the hill there was a crown of bright lights. He rose from the boulder and flexed his broad shoulders as he jumped, bringing his knees to his muscled chest with ease before racing up the dirt-packed path of the hill as the darkness claimed the skies.

At the top everything intensified. The music. The smell of richly seasoned foods being cooked in the outdoor kitchen. The bright lights adorning the wooden planks of the large pergola. And the laughter and voices of his extended family all settled around the carved wooden benches, or dancing in the center of the tiled patio. The scent of the fruit of the towering royal palm trees filled the air as the firm trunks seemed gathered around the small farming property to offer privacy.

The three-bedroom villa with its one lone bathroom and barely an acre of land was modest in comparison with his beachfront estate, but it was here among his cousins, with the night pulsing with the sounds of music and laughter, that he felt warmth and comfort.

Mi familia.

He came to a stop, just barely shaded by the darkness, and looked at his petite, dark-haired mother whose brown complexion hinted at the history of a large majority of Dominicans having African ancestry due to the slave trade of the early 1700s. She stood before a rustic wood-fired oven, stirring the ingredients in a cast-iron pot as she moved her hips and shoulders in sync to the music. He chuckled as she sang along with Cardi B's part of the song and raised the large wooden spoon she held in the air.

Everyone cheered and clapped when she tackled the rap part, as well.

Esmerelda Diaz was his mother and everyone's beloved. Although only forty-nine, she was the last of the Diaz elders. The baby girl who grew up to lead their descendants.

His mother turned and spotted him standing there. Her dark, doe-shaped eyes lit up as if she didn't have her own suite on his estate and had not fixed him *pescado con coco* for lunch. His stomach grumbled at the thought of the snapper fish cooked in coconut sauce.

"Chance!" she exclaimed, waving him over. *"Mira. Mira. Mira."*

The nine members of his extended family all looked over to him and waved as they greeted him. His cousin Carlos, a rotund, strong man in his late twenties, came over to press an ice-cold green bottle of Presidente beer in his hand as he slapped him soundly on the back in greeting.

This was the home of Carlos, his wife and four small children. He owned and operated farmlands of just three acres only a few hundred yards from the villa and was proud of his work, like many other Dominican farmers, providing locally grown fruits and vegetables and taking care of his family. Chance respected his cousin's hard work ethic and enjoyed plenty of his harvest during his time in the country. In kind, he knew his family respected him for the success he had made of his life back in the Estados Unidos.

"Tough day?" Chance asked.

Carlos shrugged one shoulder. "Same as always. And you, *primo*?" he asked with a playful side-eye and a chuckle before he took a swig of his own beer.

Chance laughed. His days of finance work and the development of his app had never been physically hard, and now that he just served as a consultant to the firm that'd purchased his app, the majority of his time was spent maintaining his toned physique and enjoying the fruits of his labor. Life was good, with his private jet, his estate in Cabrera and his permanent one in Alpine, New Jersey, and the ability to do whatever he wanted, whenever he chose. And during this time of his life, he chose to travel, enjoy fine food and wine, and spare himself nothing.

His days of struggling were over. As were his days of feeling less than for having less than.

"Excuse me, I'm starving," he said, moving past his younger cousin to reach his mother.

She smiled up at him before turning her attention back to stirring the pot.

"Sancocho de mariscos," he said in pleasure at the sight of the shellfish stew rich with shrimp, lobster, scallops, garlic, plantains, pumpkin and potatoes.

"Sí," Esmerelda said, tapping the spoon on the edge of the pot before setting it atop a folded towel on the wooden table next to the stove.

Living in a town directly off the Atlantic Ocean had its privileges. Although Chance was no stranger to traditional Dominican cooking. On her rare days off, his mother would go shopping and spend the day cooking and then freezing meals for him to enjoy while she was at work.

"Como estas?" she asked in rapid Spanish as she reached up to lightly tap the bottom of his chin with her fingertips.

"I'm fine," he assured her.

She shrugged one shoulder and slightly turned her lips downward as she tilted her head to the side. Translation? She didn't agree with him, but so be it.

The radio began to blare "Borracho de Amor" by Jose Manuel Calderon, and Chance was thankful. His mother gave a little yelp of pleasure and clapped rapidly at the sound of one of her favorite songs from the past before she grabbed the hand of her nephew Victor and began dancing the traditional *bachata*.

Chance took a seat at a wooden table and placed his beer on it as he watched his mother, alive and happy among her culture and her family. But as everyone focused on their dance, his attention was on the words of the song. As was common with traditional *bachata* music that was about heartache, pain and betrayal, it was a song of a man who turned to drinking after the heartache and pain caused by a woman's scorn. It was said that the tortured emotions displayed in the song fueled *bachata* dancers to release those emotions through dance.

Chance knew about heartache all too well.

His gut tightened into a knot at the memory of his former fiancée, Helena Guzman, running off with her lover and leaving him at the altar. In the beautiful blond-haired Afro-Cuban attorney he'd thought he found the one woman to spend his life with. She'd even agreed to give up her career as a successful attorney to travel the world with him.

But he'd been wrong. And made a fool of.

His anger at her was just beginning to thaw. His mother referred to her only as "Ese Rubio Diablo." The blond devil.

Cabrera had helped him to heal.

But now I'm headed home.

This celebration was his family's farewell to both him and his mother.

The daughter of his best friend since their days at Dalton, Alek Ansah, and his wife, Alessandra, had been born and he'd been appointed her godfather. He'd yet to see her in person; photos and FaceTime had sufficed, but now it was time to press kisses to the cheek of his godchild and do his duty at her upcoming baptism.

In the morning they would board his private plane and fly back to the States. She would return to the house he purchased for her in New Jersey, and he would be back at his estate in a house he'd foolishly thought he would share with his wife and their family one day.

Chance looked over into the shadowed trunks of the trees that surrounded the property as his thoughts went back to the day he was supposed to wed the woman he loved…

"I'm sorry, Chance, but I can't marry you," Helena said, standing before him in her custom wed-

ding dress and veil as they stood in the vestibule of the church.

For a moment, Chance just eyed her. His emotions raced one behind the other quickly, almost colliding, like dominoes set up to fall. Confusion. Fear. Pain.

"I am in love with someone else," she said, her eyes filled with her regret.

Anger.

Visions of her loving and being loved by another man burned him to his core like a branding. The anger spread across his body slowly, seeming to infuse every bit of him as the truth of her betrayal set in.

"How could you do this, Helena?" he asked, turning from her with a slash of his hand through the air, before immediately turning back with his blazing fury.

And his hurt.

That infuriated him further.

"How long?" he asked, his voice stiff.

"Chance," Helena said.

"Who is he?"

She held up her hands. "That is irrelevant," she said. "It is over. It is what it is, Chance."

"Who?" he asked again, unable to look at her.

"My ex, Jason."

The heat of his anger was soon replaced with the chill of his heart symbolically turning to stone. He stepped back from her, his jaw tightly clenched. "To hell with you," he said in a low and harsh whisper.

Long after she had gathered her voluminous skirt in her hands and rushed from the church to run down the stairs, straight into the waiting car of her lover,

Chance had stood there in the open doorway of the church and fought to come to grips with the explosive end of their whirlwind courtship.

Chance shook his head a bit to clear it of the memory, hating that nearly eight months later it still stung. The betrayal. The hurt. The dishonor.

Damn.

"*Baila conmigo*, Chance."

He turned his head to find Sofía, the best friend of Carlos's wife, extending her hand to him as she danced in place. She was a brown-skinned beauty with bright eyes, a warm smile and a shapely frame that drew the eye of men with ease. They had enjoyed one passionate night together a few months ago after a night of dancing, but both agreed it could be no more than that, with his plans to return to the States. And his desire to not be in another relationship.

Accepting her offer, he rose to his feet and took her hand, pulling her body closer to his as they danced the *bachata*. "You remember what happened the last time we danced?" he teased her, looking down into her lively eyes.

Sofía gave him a sultry smile before spinning away and then back to him. "I can't think of a better way to say goodbye," she said.

Chance couldn't agree more.

"Lord, help me get through this day."

Ngozi Johns cast a quick pleading look up to the fall skies as she zipped up the lightly quilted crimson running jacket she wore with a black long-sleeved T-shirt, leggings and sneakers. The sun was just beginning to rise, and the early morning air was crisp. She inhaled it deeply as she stretched her limbs and bent her frame into a few squats before jogging down the double level of stairs of her parents' five-bedroom, six-bathroom brick Colonial.

Her sneakered feet easily ate up the distance around the circular drive and down the long paved driveway to reach Azalea Street—like every street in the small but affluent town of Passion Grove, New Jersey, it was named after flowers.

Ngozi picked up the pace, barely noticing the estates she passed with the homes all set back from the street. Or the wrought iron lamppost on each corner breaking up the remaining darkness. Or the lone school in town, Passion Grove Middle School, on Rose Lane. Or the entire heart-shaped lake in the center of the town that residents lounged around in the summer and skated on in the winter.

She waved to local author Lance Millner, who was in the center of the body of water in his fishing boat, as he was every morning. The only time he was to be seen by his Passion Grove neighbors was during his time in the water, tossing his reel into the lake, or the rare occasions he visited the upscale grocery store on Main Street. In the distance, on the other side of the lake, was his large brick eight-bedroom home with curtains shielding the light from entering through any of the numerous windows. He lived alone and rarely had any guests. The man was as successful at being a recluse as he was at being a *New York Times* bestselling author.

He waved back.

It was a rushed move, hard and jerking, and looked more like he was swatting away a nagging fly than giving a greeting.

Ngozi smiled as she continued her run. With one movement that was as striking as flipping the middle finger, he confirmed his reputation as a lone wolf with no time to waste for anyone. When he did venture from his lakeside estate, his tall figure was always garbed in a field jacket and a boonie hat that shaded his face.

Passion Grove was the perfect place to come to enjoy high-scale living but avoid the bustle, noise and congestion of larger cities. Home to many wealthy young millennials, the town's population was under two thousand, with fewer than three hundred homes, each on an average of five or more acres. Very unlike Harlem, New York. She had enjoyed living in the city, soaking in the vibrancy of its atmosphere and culture and the beauty of its brownstones and its brown-skinned people—until a year ago. A year to the date, in fact.

When everything changed.

"Damn," she swore in a soft whisper as she shook her head, hoping to clear it.

Of her sadness. Her guilt.

Ngozi ran harder, wishing it were as easy to outrace her feelings.

It wasn't.

She came to a stop on the corner of Marigold and Larkspur, pressing her hand to her heaving chest as her heart continued to race, even though she did not. She grimaced as she released a shaky breath. She knew the day would be hard.

It had been only a year.

Ngozi bit her bottom lip and began jogging in place to maintain the speed of her heartbeat before she finally gathered enough strength to push aside her worries and continue her morning run. She needed to finish. She needed to know there was true hope that one day her guilt and remorse would no longer hinder her.

She continued her run, noticing that outside of the echo of her colorful sneakers pounding on the pavement, the chirp of birds and errant barks of dogs occasionally broke the silence. With the town comprising sizable estates that were all set back three hundred or more feet from the streets—per a local ordinance—the noise was at a minimum.

"Good morning, Counselor."

Ngozi looked over her shoulder to find the town's police chief standing on the porch of the Victorian home that had once served as the town's mercantile during the early days of its creation in the 1900s. For the last fifty years, it had served as the police station and was more than sufficient for the small town. She turned, jogging in place as she looked up at the tall and sturdy blond man who looked as if his uniform was a size—maybe two—too small. "Morning, Chief

Ransom," she greeted him as she checked her pulse against the Fitbit. "Care to join me?"

He threw his head back and laughed, almost causing his brown Stetson hat to fall from his head. "No, no, no," he said, looking at her with a broad smile that caused the slight crinkles at the corners of his brown eyes to deepen. He patted his slightly rounded belly. "My better half loves everything just as it is."

Eloise, his wife, was as thin as a broomstick. Opposites clearly attracted because it was clear to all that they were deeply in love. The couple resided in the lone apartment in the entire town—the one directly above the police station. It was a perk of accepting the position as chief. It would be absurd to expect a public servant to afford one of the costly estates of Passion Grove—all valued at seven figures or more.

"You have any future clients for me?" Ngozi asked, biting her inner cheek to keep from smiling.

"In Passion Grove?" the chief balked. "*No* way."

She shrugged both her shoulders. "Just thought I'd ask," she said, running backward before she waved and turned to race forward down the street.

As a successful New York criminal defense attorney, Ngozi Johns was familiar with the tristate area's high-crime places. Passion Grove definitely was not counted among them. The chief had only two part-time deputies to assist him when there was a rare criminal act in the town, and so far that was limited to driving violations, not curbing a dog, jaywalking or the occasional shoplifting from the grocery store or lone upscale boutique by a thrill-seeking, bored housewife.

There were no apartment buildings or office buildings. No public transportation. Only stop signs, no traffic lights. There were strict limitations on commercial activity to maintain the small-town feel. Keeping up its beautiful aesthetic was a priority, with large pots on each street corner filled with plants or colorful perennial floras.

Like the police station, the less than dozen stores lining one side of Main Street were small converted homes that were relics from the town's incorporation in the early 1900s. She jogged past the gourmet grocery store that delivered, a few high-end boutiques, a dog groomer and the concierge service that supplied luxuries not available in town. Each business was adorned with crisp black awnings. She crossed the street to ignore the temptation of fresh-brewed coffee and fresh-baked goods wafting from La Boulangerie, the bakery whose delicacies were as sinfully delicious as the store was elegantly decorated like a French bistro.

She appreciated the serenity and beauty as she reached the garden that bloomed with colorful fall flowers, and soon was at the elaborate bronze sign welcoming everyone to Passion Grove. She tapped the back of it with gusto before taking a deep breath and starting the run back home.

Ngozi successfully kept her thoughts filled with upcoming depositions or cases. By the time she turned up the drive and spotted her parents' sprawling home, the sun was blazing in the sky and some of the chill had left the morning air. She felt less gloomy.

Thank you, God.

"Good morning, Ngozi."

Her heart pounded more from surprise at the sound of her father's deep voice than the run. She forced a pleasant smile and turned in the foyer to find her tall father, Horace Vincent, with deep brown skin that she'd inherited and low-cut silver hair, standing in the open door to his office. He was still in his silk pajamas, but files were in hand and he eyed her over the rim of his spectacles.

"Good morning, Daddy," she said, walking across the hardwood floors to press a tender kiss to his cheek. "I just finished my run."

Horace was a retired corporate and banking attorney who started Vincent and Associates Law over forty years ago. It was one of the top five hundred law firms in the country—a huge accomplishment for an African American man—and Ngozi was proud to be one of the firm's top criminal trial attorneys.

"Ngozi!"

The urge to wince rose quickly in her, but Ngozi was well practiced in hiding her true feelings from her parents. "Yes, Mama?" she asked, following her father into his office to find her mother leaning against the edge of the massive wooden desk in the center of the room. She was also still in her nightwear, a satin red floor-length gown and matching robe.

Even in her seventies, Valerie "Val" Vincent was the epitome of style, poise and confidence. Her silver bob was sleek and modern. She exercised daily and stuck to a vegan diet to maintain her size-eight figure. Her caramel-brown skin, high cheekbones, intelligent brown eyes and full mouth were beautiful even before her routine application of makeup. She was constantly mistaken for being in her fifties, but was regally proud of every year of her age.

And she was as brilliant as she was beautiful, having cultivated a career as a successful trial attorney before becoming a congresswoman and garnering respect for her political moves.

"I know today is difficult for you, Ngozi," Val said, her eyes soft and filled with the concern of a mother for her child.

As her soul withered, Ngozi kept her face stoic and her eyes vacant. She never wanted to be the cause for worry in her parents. "I'm fine, Mama," she lied with ease.

Her parents shared a look.

Ngozi diverted her eyes from them. They landed on the wedding photo sitting on the corner of her father's desk. She fought not to release a heavy breath. The day she wed Dennis Johns, she had put on a facade as well and played the role of the perfectly happy bride vowing to love the man she'd met in law school.

Until death do us part.

After only four years.

She was a widow at twenty-nine.

She blinked rapidly to keep the tears at bay.

"We want you to know there's no rush to leave," her father began.

Ngozi shifted her gaze back to them, giving them both a reassuring smile that was as false as the hair on the head of a cheap doll. It was well practiced.

I'm always pretending.

"When we suggested you move back home after Dennis's…passing, your mother and I were happy you accepted the offer, and we hope you'll stay awhile," Horace continued.

"Of course, Daddy," she said, widening her smile. "Who wants to leave a mansion with enough staff to make you think you're on vacation? I ain't going nowhere."

They both smiled, her show of humor seeming to bring them relief.

It was a pattern she was all too familiar with.

How would it feel to tell them no?

Her eyes went to the other frame on her father's desk and landed on the face of her older brother, Haaziq. More death.

She winced, unable to hide what his passing meant for her. Not just the loss of her brother from her life, but the role she accepted as defender of her parents' happiness. Losing their son, her brother, in an accidental drowning at the tender age of eight had deeply affected their family. Little six-year-old Ngozi, with her thick and coarse hair in long ponytails and glasses, had never wanted to be a hassle or let down her parents because of their grief. She'd always worn a bright smile, learned to pretend everything was perfect and always accepted that whatever they wanted for her was the right course of action.

"Let's all get ready for work, and I'm sure breakfast will be on the table by the time we're ready to go and conquer the world," Val said, lovingly stroking Horace's chin before rising to come over and squeeze her daughter's hand.

At the thought of another meal, Ngozi wished she had dipped inside the bakery, enjoyed the eye candy that was Bill the Blond and Buff Baker, and gobbled down one of the decadent treats he baked while resembling Paul Walker.

Bzzzzzz.

Ngozi reached for her iPhone from the small pocket of her jacket. "Excuse me," she said to her parents before turning and leaving the office.

She smiled genuinely as she answered the call. "The early baby gets the mother's milk, huh?" she teased, jogging up the wooden staircase with wrought iron railings with a beautiful scroll pattern.

"Right." Alessandra Dalmount-Ansah laughed. "The early bird has nothing on my baby. Believe that."

Alessandra was the co-CEO of the billion-dollar conglomerate the Ansah Dalmount Group, along with her husband, Alek Ansah. Ngozi served as her personal attorney, while corporate matters were handled by other attorneys at Vincent and Associates Law. The women had become closer when Ngozi successfully represented Alessandra when she was mistakenly arrested during a drug raid. She'd been in the wrong place at the absolute worst time, trying to save her cousin Marisa Martinez during a major drug binge.

"How's my godchild?" Ngozi asked, crossing the

stylishly decorated family room on the second level to reach one of the three-bedroom suites flanking the room.

"Full. Her latch game is serious."

They laughed.

The line went quiet just as Ngozi entered her suite and kicked off her sneakers before holding the phone between her ear and her shoulder as she unzipped and removed the lightweight jacket.

"How are you?" Alessandra asked, her concern for her friend clear.

"I'm good," Ngozi said immediately, as she dropped down onto one of the four leather recliners in the sitting area before the fireplace and the flat-screen television on the wall above it.

Liar, liar.

She closed her eyes and shook her head.

Then she heard a knock.

"Alessandra, can I call you back? Someone's at my door," she said, rising to her feet and crossing the room.

"Sure. See you at the baptism Sunday."

"Absolutely."

Ngozi ended the call and opened the door. Reeds, her parents' house manager, stood before her holding a tray with a large bronzed dome cover. She smiled at the man of average height with shortbread complexion, more freckles than stars in the sky and graying brownish-red hair in shoulder-length locks. "One day my mother is going to catch you," she said as she took the tray from him and removed the lid to reveal buttered grits, bacon, scrambled eggs and toast.

He shrugged and chuckled. "The rest of the staff wouldn't know what to do without me after all these years."

"I *know* that's right," Ngozi said with a playful wink.

"Just remember to at least eat the bowl of fruit at breakfast," Reeds said before he turned and began to whistle some jazzy tune. He stopped in the middle of the family room to glance back. "*Or* you could just tell your mother you're not vegan. Your choice."

Ngozi ignored his advice and stepped back into the room, knocking the door with her hip to push it closed.

Chapter 2

The day of reckoning is here.

Chance splashed his face with water and pressed his hands to his cheeks before wiping the corner of his eyes with his thumb. He stood tall before the sink and eyed his reflection in the large leather-framed mirror above it. He released a heavy breath and studied himself, rubbing his hand over his low-cut fade haircut.

Today he would face his friends for the first time since what was supposed to be his wedding day. With the last bit of pride and bravado he could muster, Chance had stood before all those people and admitted that the wedding was called off. The swell of gasps of shock and whispers had filled the church as he strode down the aisle with nearly every eye locked on his stoic expression. He would admit to no one the embarrassment he felt, and didn't allow his head to sink one bit until he left the church.

He had instructed Alek to have the wedding planner, Olivia Joy, turn the reception into a party, but he had not attended the event. The idea of being pitied or ridiculed by Helena's betrayal was too strong for him to swallow. He spent what was supposed to be his wedding night ignoring all attempts at communicating with him as he nursed a bottle of pricey Dos Lunas Grand Reserve tequila, stewed in his anger and envisioned Helena being bedded by her lover.

Early that next morning, with a hangover from hell, he boarded his private jet and flew to Cabrera with no foreseeable plans to return. His consultant work for the same firm that purchased his app could be handled from anywhere in the world with Wi-Fi. All he knew was he had to get away. So he did.

Now I'm back.

He eyed his reflection, hating the nerves and anxiousness he felt.

It took him back to his school days as a poor brown-skinned Latino kid from the Bronx trying his best not to feel less than around students who were predominantly white and absolutely from wealthy families.

He flexed his arms and bent his head toward each of his shoulders, instinctively trying to diminish those feelings from his youth. "Let's get this over with," he mumbled under his breath, removing his towel and

drying his body before tossing it over the smoothed
edge of the cast concrete in the center of the dark and
modern bathroom.

He quickly swiped on his deodorant and lightly
sprayed on cologne from one of the ten bottles sitting
on a long ebony wood tray in the space between the
large tray sinks atop the concrete vanity.

Naked, he strode across the heated marble floors
and through the opening in the tinted-glass wall to
his loft-style bedroom suite. His motorized open-front
closets lined the entire wall behind his king-size Mon-
arch Vi-Spring bed, but the suit he'd already selected
was laid across one of the custom chaise longues at
the foot of it. His long and thick member swayed
across his thighs as he moved to pull on his snug
boxers, having to adjust it to comfort before he finished dressing in silk socks, his off-white wool-silk
suit and a matching open-neck shirt. The fit against
his athletic frame spoke to its custom tailoring and
his desire for both quality and style.

Not wanting to run late, he hurriedly selected one
of a dozen watches to buckle around his wrist while
slipping on shoes that were almost as comfortable
as his bed.

Life was good when it came to the creature com-
forts. The days of squeaky rubber-sole shoes from
the dollar store were over.

I hated to walk in 'em, he remembered. *Felt like
everyone heard me coming.*

He rushed through his opulent two-story villa-
style mansion, which sat on two gated acres in Al-

pine, New Jersey, styled in muted tasteful decor with vibrant pops of color that were a testament to his dynamic Latino culture. Chance lived alone in the six-bedroom luxury home, and he usually kept music or his 4K televisions on to break the silence. Hip-hop from the 1990s played from the sound system, and he rapped along to Big Daddy Kane's "Ain't No Half-Steppin'" as he grabbed his keys from beside the glass-blown structures of nude women atop the table in the center of the foyer.

Soon he was out the double front doors and behind the wheel of his black-on-black Ferrari 488 Pista, taking I-280 to Passion Grove. He drove the super-car with ease with one hand, effortlessly switching lanes on the interstate as he lightly tapped his fist against his knee to the music playing. The commute was hassle-free because it was Sunday morning, and he was grateful as he finally guided the vehicle down the exit ramp and made his way through the small town. He didn't think he could find an upscale town more laid-back than Alpine, but Passion Grove proved him wrong.

A city without traffic lights in 2018?

Chance felt bored already. He still found it hard to believe that his fun-loving best friend, Alek—who was born into a billionaire dynasty—chose the small town to live in after jet-setting all over the world.

Real love will make you do unexpected things.

His and Helena's plans had been to travel the world and explore new adventures after they were wed.

And look how that turned out.

His hand gripped the steering wheel, lightening the color of his skin across his knuckles. He was glad to finally make it to Alek and Alessandra's, accelerating up the private mile-long paved street leading to the expansive twenty-five-acre estate until he reached the twelve-foot-tall wrought iron gate with the letter *D* in bronzed scroll in the center.

Alessandra had inherited the estate upon the death of her father, Frances Dalmount, who co-owned the billionaire conglomerate the Ansah Dalmount Group, along with Alek's father, the late Kwame Ansah. When Alessandra and Alek wed last year, they'd decided to make the Passion Grove estate their main home, while maintaining both his Manhattan and London penthouse apartments, and the vacation estate they built together on their private island in upstate New York.

After getting checked in by security via video surveillance, Chance drove through the open gates and soon was pulling up to the massive stone French Tudor. He hopped out and pressed a tip into the hand of one of the valets his friends were using for the day to park the vehicles.

He jogged up the stairs and accepted a flute of champagne from the tray being held by a servant. "Thank you," he said with a nod of his head as he entered the foyer through the open double doors.

"Thanks so much."

Chance paused and turned at the soft voice. He froze with his drink still raised to his mouth as he eyed the woman over the rim of the crystal flute. His heart began to pound, and his breath caught in his throat. *Well, damn...*

She was beautiful. Tall and shapely with skin as dark and smooth as melted chocolate. Long and loose waves of her beyond-shoulder-length ebony hair framed her oval face with high cheekbones, bright and clear brown doe-like eyes, and a nose bringing forth a regal beauty similar to the women of Somalia. The long-sleeved white lace dress she wore clung to her frame with a V-neck highlighting her small but plump breasts, and a wide skirt above long shapely legs. Her gold accessories gave her skin further sheen.

As she walked past the valet with a soft reserved smile, the wind shifted, causing her hair to drift back from her face as she moved with confident long strides that flexed the toned muscles of her legs and caused the skirt of her dress to flounce around her thighs. He couldn't take his eyes off her and had no desire to do so. She was a treat, and the very sight of her as she easily jogged up the stairs made him hunger for her.

He smiled like a wolf behind his flute as his eyes dipped to take her in from head to delicious feet displayed in open-toe sandals with tassels that were sexy.

Who is she?

He felt excited with each step that brought her closer to him. When she paused to take her own flute of champagne, his hawk-like eyes locked on how the flesh of her mouth pressed against the crystal, leaving a light stain of her lip gloss on the glass.

Who is she? And does she want to leave with me later?

The prospect of that made his return to the States completely worth it.

"There you are, Chance."

With regret, he turned from his temptress. "Here I am," he agreed, genuinely smiling at Alessandra Dalmount-Ansah as she walked up to him, looking beautiful in a white light georgette dress with perfect tailoring.

She grabbed his upper arms lightly as she rose up on the tips of her shoes to press a kiss to his cheek. "Welcome home, Chance," she said with warmth, looking up at him with sympathetic eyes as she raised a hand to lightly tap his chin. "You good?"

He nodded, hating the unease he felt. *How much more of this pity will there be today?* he wondered, purposefully turning from her to eye the beauty in peach as she stepped inside the foyer.

Her eyes landed on his, and he gave that lingering stare and slow once-over that was nothing but pure appreciation and a desire to know more. Her brows arched a bit and her mouth gaped as she gave him the hint of a smile that was just enough to give him

"Hey, Ngozi," Alessandra said, moving
to kiss her cheek in welcome.

*So, this is Ngozi? Alessandr
attorney. Brains and beauty.* Ju
said to him so many times.

Her eyes left him, and Ch

taking a sip of the champagne he instantly recognized as Armand de Brignac.

"That's right, you two have never met," Alessandra said, reaching for one of Ngozi's hands and then one of Chance's. "Chance Castillo, godfather, meet Ngozi Johns, godmother."

She pressed their hands together.

Their eyes met.

As they clasped hands, Chance stroked the pulse at her wrist with his thumb, enjoying how it pounded. It matched his own.

Ngozi felt breathless.

Her first sight of Chance Castillo as she stepped inside the house had made her entire body tingle with excitement. He was tall with an athletic frame that could not be denied in his tailored suit. His stance as he stood there eyeing her over the rim of his glass spoke of unleashed power. A man. A strong man built for pleasure. Not just handsome, with his medium-brown complexion and angular features softened by lips and intensified by his deep-set eyes, the shadow of a beard and his low-cut ebony hair…but intriguing. Something about him had instantly drawn her in. Excited her. Made her curious. Forced her to wonder, *Who is he?*

And now, as Ngozi stood there with her hand mingly engulfed by his with his thumb gently her pulse, she shivered and sought control Her pulse. Her heartbeat. Her breaths.

The pounding of the sweet fleshy bud nestled between the lips of her core. *Damn.*

All of it surprised her. Never had she had such an instantaneous reaction to a man before.

Needing to be released from the spell he cast upon her, Ngozi pulled her hand from his and forced a smile that she hoped didn't look as awkward as it felt. "Nice to finally meet, Mr. Castillo," she said, proud of her restored cool composure.

It was all a sham, and she deserved an award for the performance.

"Chance," he offered, sliding the hand she once held into the pocket of his slacks.

"Right this way, y'all," Alessandra said, leading them across the stately round foyer, past the staircase and down the hall into the family room, where the glass doors were retracted, creating an entertaining space that flowed with people lounging inside or outside on the patio or around the pool.

Alek spotted them and excused himself from a couple he was talking with to cross the room to them. It was similar to watching a politician or other public figure as he spoke to each person who stopped him while still moving toward them. The man was charismatic.

Ngozi took a sip of her champagne as she glanced at Alessandra over the rim. The look in her friend's eyes as she watched her husband was nothing but love. She'd found her happily-ever-after.

A twinge of pain radiated across her chest, and Ngozi forced herself to smile in spite of it.

"Careful, Ngozi," Alessandra said, holding out her arm in front of her. "Don't get in the way of this bro love, girl."

Ngozi looked on as Chance took a few strides to meet Alek. The men, equally handsome, confident and strong in build, clasped hands and then moved in for a brotherly hug complete with a solid slap of their hand against the other's back. It barely lasted a moment, but it was clear they were close.

As the men talked quietly to one another, Ngozi eyed Chance's profile, surprised by her reaction to him. And she still felt a tingle of awareness and a thrill that ruffled her feathers. He smiled at something Alek said, and her stomach clenched as a handsome face was instantly transformed into a beautiful one.

"He looks happy," Alessandra said softly to herself.

Ngozi glanced over at her, seeing the hope on her face that her words were true. She remembered Alessandra explaining Chance's absence because he had been left at the altar by his fiancée and was in the Dominican Republic recovering from his heartache. That had been nearly nine months ago.

What woman would leave him behind?

Ngozi had never asked for any more details than Alessandra offered, but that was before she'd seen him. Now a dozen or more questions flew to mind with ease. Her curiosity was piqued.

"I'm going up to get the baby," Alessandra said. "Be right back."

Ngozi glanced around the room, raising her flute

in toast to those she knew professionally or personally. When her eyes landed back on the men, she found Chance's eyes on her. She gasped a little. Her pulse raced.

He gave her a wolfish grin—slow and devastating—as he locked his gaze with hers. They made their way toward her, and Ngozi forced herself to look away as she felt a shiver race down her spine.

"I wanted to finally greet you, Ngozi," Alek said.

She looked up at him with a smile. "I thought I was invisible," she teased, presenting her cheek for a kiss as she pretended Chance was not standing there, as well.

"Chance told me Alessandra already made the introductions between you two," Alek said.

She stiffened her back and glanced up at Chance. "Yes, it's nice to finally put a face to the name," she said.

"Same here," he agreed. "Especially since we're sharing godparent duties."

"Right, right," she agreed with a genuine smile. "We'll rock, paper, scissors for overnight stays."

He opened his mouth and then closed it, biting his bottom lip as if to refrain himself. He shared a brief look with Alek, who then shook his head and chuckled.

And she knew—she just *knew*—Chance was going to say they could have overnights together.

"Really, fellas?" she asked, eyeing them both like a teacher reprimanding naughty schoolboys.

"What?" they both asked innocently in unison.

Ngozi was surprised to see Alek, normally severe and businesslike, standing before her with mirth in his eyes. "So, we all have that one thing or one person—a vice—that makes us different. Today, Alek Ansah," she said before turning to face Chance, "I have met yours."

Chance's smile broadened as he looked down at her. "And what—or who—makes you different, Ngozi Johns?"

She loved how her name sounded on his lips. "Oh, is there something about me that needs fixing?" she asked, forcing herself not to quiver under his intense stare as she met it with one of her own.

"From what I can see, not one damn thing," Chance responded with ease, his voice deep and masculine.

"On *that* note," Alek said, clearing his throat as he looked from one to the other, "I'll take my leave."

And he did, leaving them alone.

"Ngozi!"

At the sound of her name, Ngozi broke their stare and turned to find Marisa Martinez standing beside her. She gave the petite woman with a wild mane of shoulder-length curly hair a warm smile. "It's good to see you, Marisa," she said, her eyes taking in the clarity in the woman's eyes and feeling sweet relief.

The former party girl who lived hard and fast off the allowance she received from the Dalmount dynasty had developed an addiction to alcohol and drugs that put both her and Alessandra's freedom in jeopardy. As the head of the family, Alessandra felt it her obligation to guide and protect the entire clan made up of her two aunts, Leonora Dalmount and

Brunela Martinez, her cousin Victor Dalmount and his bride, Elisabetta, and Marisa, Brunela's daughter. That sense of duty had led Alessandra to seek out Marisa at a house party and to get caught in the middle of a police drug raid.

Ngozi was called on by her client to represent them both. The charges were dropped, but Alessandra had forced Marisa to either attend the long-term rehab program Ngozi arranged or be disowned.

Marisa chose the former, and six months later, she'd returned drug-free.

"I just wanted to thank you for everything you did to help me," Marisa said, before lifting up on her toes to give Ngozi an impromptu hug.

"Well, I thank you for not letting my hard work go to waste," she said, returning the hug. "You look good."

Marisa released her. "I feel better," she said, her eyes serious before she forced a smile and walked away with one last squeeze of Ngozi's hand.

She watched her walk over to join her mother and aunt Leonora by the fireplace. With her work as a criminal attorney who insisted on pro bono work and tough cases, Ngozi was well acquainted with thankful clients.

"I've heard you're one of the best attorneys on the East Coast."

Him.

Ngozi took a sip of her champagne as she eyed him with an arched brow. "Just the East Coast?" she teased.

He chuckled.

"I'm kidding," she rushed to say, reaching out to grasp his wrist.

His pulse pounded against her fingertips. She released him.

"La tentadora," Chance said.

The temptress.

Her entire body flushed with warmth.

Chance was Dominican on his mother's side, and like many other Afro-Latinos did appear to be what was standardly thought of as such. Much like Laz Alonso, Victor Cruz and Carmelo Anthony.

"Me das demasiado crédito," she said, loving the surprise that filled his deep brown eyes at her using his native tongue to tell him that he gave her too much credit.

"Ah! ¿Tu hablas español?" he asked.

"Yes, I speak Spanish," she answered with a nod.

"¿Pero alguna vez te ha susurrado un hombre en español mientras te hace el amor?"

Ngozi gasped in surprise and pleasure and excitement at his question of whether a man had whispered to her in Spanish while making love. She recovered quickly. "No," she answered him, before easing past his strong build and imposing presence to leave.

"Usted tiene algo que esperar," Chance said from behind her.

Then you have something to look forward to.

Chance Castillo.

She gave in to her own temptation and glanced back at him over her shoulder. He had turned his attention to greeting Alek's younger brother, Naim. She pressed her fingertips to her neck as she turned away, admitting regret that his attention was no longer on her.

In truth, she couldn't remember feeling that affected by a man in a long, long time.

She pursed her lips and released a stream of air, intending to calm herself.

Ngozi stopped a male waiter and set her near-empty flute on the tray. "Thank you," she said. Her stomach rumbled, and she looked around with a slight frown, hoping no one had heard it. Quickly, she turned and tapped the shoulder of the waiter. "Is there another one like you with a tray of hors d'oeuvres? A sista is hungry."

He chuckled and shook his head. "Not yet," he said. "The food will be served after the ceremonies."

Damn. Ngozi checked her platinum watch as he walked away.

She crossed the room and made her way outdoors. During the day, the September air was still pleasant. It was the early mornings and late nights that brought on a chill that reminded her summer was drawing to an end.

As she neared the Olympic-sized pool, she felt an urge to jump in and sink beneath the crystal clear depths to swim to the other end and back. Instead, she settled for slipping off one of her sandals to dip her toes in the water, causing it to ripple outward.

Dennis loved to swim.

She felt sadness, closing her eyes as she remembered his looking back at her over his shoulder before he dived into the deep end of her parents' pool back in some of the rare moments of free time they had during law school.

She smiled a bit, remembering how happy they were then.

That was a long time ago.

"Excuse me, Ms. Johns."

She was surprised by the same waiter who took her drink, now standing beside her with a sandwich on his tray.

"Courtesy of Olga, the house manager, per the request of Mr. Castillo," he said.

Ngozi looked up and bit back a smile at Chance standing in the open doorway, raising his flute to her in a silent toast. Her stomach rumbled again as she bowed her head to him in gratitude. She assumed he had overhead her conversation with the waiter.

"One sec, please," she said, holding the man's wrist to keep her balance as she slipped her damp foot back into her sandal.

Once done, she took the sandwich and cloth napkin from him and bit into it. Her little grunt was pure pleasure at the taste of seasoned and warmed roast beef with a gooey cheese and a tasty spread on the bread. "Thank you," she said to him around the food, with a complete lack of the decorum she had been taught by her parents.

"No problem."

As he walked away to finish his duties, Ngozi turned her back to the house and enjoyed the view of the manicured lawns to avoid people watching her eat.

"Ngozi."

Him.

Her body went on high alert. Every pulse point on her pounded. *What is wrong with me? Am I in heat?*

"Yes?" she said, patting the corners of her mouth with the napkin before turning to face him. *Wow. He's fine.*

Chance was nursing his second glass of champagne and squinting from the sun of the late summer season as he eyed her.

"You shouldn't drink on an empty stomach," she said, offering him the other half of the sandwich still on the saucer.

He eyed it and then her. "My appetite isn't for food, Ngozi," he said before taking another deep sip of his drink.

"The only thing I have for you is half of this sandwich, Mr. Castillo," she said, keeping her voice cool and even.

He chuckled.

"Akwaaba. Akwaaba. Memo o akwaaba."

They both turned to find LuLu Ansah, Alek's mother, standing in the open doorway looking resplendent in traditional African white garb with gold embroidery with a matching head wrap that was simply regal. Both the Ansah and Dalmount families surrounded her, with Alek and Alessandra beside her with the baby in Alessandra's arms. Both she and Alek looked around before they spotted Chance and Ngozi, waving them over.

They rushed to take their place, Ngozi gratefully handing the saucer and the remainder of the sandwich to one of the waiters.

"Welcome. Welcome. We welcome you," LuLu

translated, looking around at everyone gathered with a warm smile that made her eyes twinkle.

Ngozi leaned forward a bit to eye her goddaughter, who was just eight days old. She was beautiful. A perfect blend of Alek and Alessandra, with tightly coiled ebony hair and cheeks that were already round. She couldn't wait to hear her name. Alessandra had not budged in revealing it early.

"Today we are honored to officially present a new addition to our family. We will have both a religious ceremony to baptize our little beauty to ensure she is favored by God, and then an outdooring, which is a traditional Ghanaian ceremony when a baby is taken outside the home for the first time, given a name and prepared with the love and wisdom we all hope for her. Is that okay with you all?" she asked, looking around at the faces of everyone in attendance with a sweet, loving expression.

People applauded or shouted out their approval.

"And so, we welcome into our world, our community, our village… Aliyah Olivia Ansah," LuLu said with pride. "May we all pray for her, guide her and love her."

Alessandra pressed a kiss to Aliyah's head, and then Alek pressed one to her temple.

She was so loved.

Ngozi was happy for them and couldn't help but smile.

Chapter 3

Two weeks later

"Congratulations, Counselor."

Ngozi finished sliding her files inside her briefcase and then raised her hand to take the one offered by the Brooklyn district attorney Walter Xavier. She had just served him a loss in his attempt to prosecute her client, an ex-FBI agent, for murder. "You didn't make it easy," she told him, matching his steady gaze with one of her own.

With one last pump of her hand and cursory nod of his head, the man who was her senior by more than thirty years turned and walked out of the courtroom with several staff members behind him.

Ngozi allowed herself a hint of a smile as she looked down into her briefcase.

"Ayyeeee! Ayyeeee! Ayyeeee!"

"Angel!" Ngozi snapped in a harsh whisper, whirling around to eye her newly appointed personal assistant at her loud cry. She found her arm raised above her head, as if she was about to hit a dance move, which took her aback. A win in the courtroom was not the same as getting "turned up" in the club.

Angel, a twentysomething beauty whose enhanced body made a button-up shirt and slacks look indecent, slowly lowered her hands and smoothed them over her hips.

"Get out," Ngozi mouthed with a stern look, seeing that other people in the court were openly eyeing them.

"What?" she mouthed back, looking confused as she picked up her fuchsia tote from her seat in the gallery and left the courtroom with a pout.

"Precious Lord," she mumbled, thankful her client had already been taken back into the holding cell by the court officers.

Ngozi often went above and beyond for her clients, including hiring a former stripper/escort as her personal assistant to meet the requirements of the probation Ngozi was able to secure. At the firm she had her own staff, clerks, paralegals and junior associates, plus an experienced legal secretary. The last thing she needed was a personal assistant—especially one like Angel, who lacked discernment.

Two weeks down, two years to go...

Ngozi gathered the rest of her items and finally left the courtroom. As she made her way through the people milling about the hallway, Angel and her junior associate, Gregor, immediately fell in behind her. Her walk was brisk. She had to get back to the Manhattan office for an appointment with a prospective new client.

She had a rule on no walking and talking outside the offices of Vincent and Associates Law, VAL, so they were quiet. Once they reached the exit on the lobby level, she saw the crowd of reporters and news cameras awaiting her. This was another huge win for her in a controversial case. She felt confident in the navy Armani cap sleeve silk charmeuse blouse, tailored blazer and wide-leg pants she wore. She had self-assuredly and correctly anticipated the win and made sure to be camera ready—which had included an early morning visit from her hairstylist/makeup artist.

"Angel, go mannequin-style and say nothing," she mumbled to the woman.

"But—"

A stare from Ngozi ended her statement before it even began.

They exited the building and then descended the double level of stairs, with Ngozi in the lead. She stopped on the street and the crowd created a semi-arc around them. "Hello, everyone. I am Ngozi Johns of Vincent and Associates Law. As you know, I am the attorney for Oscar Erscole, who has been successfully exonerated of the charges of murder that were brought against him. After a long and tenuous fight, we are thankful that the jury's discernment of the facts and the evidence presented in the case has proven what we have always asserted, which is the innocence of Mr. Erscole, who can now rebuild his life, reclaim his character and enjoy his life. Thank you all. Have a good day."

With one last cordial smile, she turned from them, ignoring the barrage of questions being fired at her as they made their way through the crowd and to their waiting black-on-black SUVs. Ngozi and Angel climbed into the rear of the first one. She pulled her iPhone from her briefcase and began checking her email. "Back to the office, please, Frank," she said to the driver, working her thumb against the touch screen to scroll.

"Now, Ms. J.?" Angel asked, sounding childlike and not twenty-one years of age.

It wasn't until the doors were closed and their tinted windows blocked them from view that Ngozi glanced over at Angel and bit the corner of her mouth to keep back her smile. "Now, Angel," she agreed.

"Ayyeeee! Ayyeeee! Ayyeeee!" Angel said, sticking out her pierced tongue and bouncing around in her seat. "Congrats, boss."

"Thanks, Angel," Ngozi said, laughing when she saw the driver, a white middle-aged man who liked the music of Frank Sinatra, stiffen in his seat and eye them in alarm via the rearview mirror.

They continued the rest of the ride in relative silence as Ngozi swiftly responded to emails and took a few calls. When the car pulled to a stop, double-parking on Park Avenue in midtown Manhattan, Ngozi gathered her things back into her briefcase as the driver came around to open the door for her. "Thank you, Frank," she said, lightly accepting the hand he offered to help her climb from the vehicle and then swiftly crossing the sidewalk with Angel on her heels and the rest of her team just behind her.

They entered the thirty-five-story beaux arts–style building complete with retail and restaurant space on the lower levels and corporate offices on the remaining thirty-three. Everything about the building spoke to its prominence and prestige. After breezing through security with their digital badges, Ngozi and the others traveled up to the twenty-second floor, where Vincent and Law Associates had occupied the entire twenty-two thousand square feet for the last twenty years, housing nearly fifty private offices, a dozen workstations, several conference rooms, a pantry, reception area complete with a waiting space and other areas essential for office work. The offices of the senior partners, including the one her father had vacated upon his retirement, were on half of the floor of the next level up.

Vincent and Associates Law was a force with which to be reckoned. Her father had begun his firm over forty years ago with his expertise in corporate and banking law. Over the years, he acquired smaller firms and attorneys with proven records of success in other specialties to expand and become a goliath in the Northeast and one of the top five hundred law firms in the country.

To know that her father spearheaded such power

and prominence made her proud each and every time she walked through the doors. It had been no easy ride for an African American man, and her respect for her father was endless. And she was determined to rightfully earn her spot as a senior partner and claim the office that sat empty awaiting her—when the time was right.

It was one of the few goals for her that they shared.

Ngozi moved with an Olivia Pope–like stride as she checked her Piaget watch. The team separated to go to their own offices or workstations in the bright white-on-white interior of the offices. Angel took her seat at a cubicle usually reserved for law interns. "Angel, order lunch. I want it in my office as soon as my meeting is over," Ngozi said as she continued her stroll across the tiled floors to her glass corner office.

"Champagne or brandy, boss?" her legal assistant, Anne, asked as she neared.

Champagne to celebrate. Brandy to commiserate.

Ngozi bit her cheek to keep from smiling. "Champagne," she said with a wink, doing a little fist pump before entering her office and waving her hand across the panel on the wall to close the automated glass door etched with her name.

She didn't have much time to marinate on the win. She took her seat behind her large glass desk and unpacked several files, her tablet and her phone from her suitcase. After checking the online record of messages sent to her by those at the reception desk, she tucked her hair behind her ear and lightly bit the tip of her nail as she stared off, away from her computer monitor, at a beam of sunlight radiating across the floor and the white leather sofa in her conversation area.

Bzzzzzz.

Her eyes went back to the screen.

A Skype call from Reception. She accepted the video option instead of the phone one. The face of Georgia, one of the firm's six receptionists, filled the screen. "Ms. Johns. Your one o'clock appointment, Mr. Castle of CIS, is here."

"Thank you, Georgia, send him in," she said.

Ngozi turned off her monitor and cleared her desk. She glanced through the glass wall of her office and then did a double take.

Him.

All her senses went haywire as she watched the handsome charmer make his way past the workstations in the center of the office with the ease of a well-trained politician. A smile here, a nod there.

And it was clear that a lot of the women—and a few of the men—were eyeing him in appreciation.

Chance Castillo was undeniably handsome, and the navy-and-olive blazer he wore with a navy button-up shirt and dark denim were stylish and sexy without even trying.

She hadn't seen him since the festivities for their goddaughter, Aliyah.

"What is he up to?" she mumbled aloud as she settled her chin in one hand and drummed the fingernails of the other against the top of her desk.

When Angel jumped up to her feet and leaned

over the wall of her cubicle, Ngozi rolled her eyes heavenward. Especially when he paused to talk to her. Soon they both looked down the length of the walkway, at her office.

His smile widened at the sight of her in the distance.

Ngozi raised her hand from the desk and waved briefly at him with a stiff smile before bending her finger to beckon him to her.

By the time he reached her office, there were many pairs of eyes on him.

She pressed the button on her desk to open the door as she rose to her feet. "Very slick of you, using the English version of Castillo, Chance," she said, extending her hand to him as she would any client—new or old.

"I didn't want to risk you canceling to avoid me," he said, taking her hand in his.

It was warm to her touch.

She gently broke the hold, reclaiming her seat. "So, you're clear on me wanting to avoid you, then?" she asked.

"Damn, you're smart," Chance said, walking around her office.

His presence made it seem smaller.

"Um, excuse, Ms. J."

Both Ngozi and Chance looked over to find Angel standing in the open doorway.

"Yes?" Ngozi asked, noting to herself that the young'un usually avoided work (in other words, coming to her office) at all costs.

"I wondered if you were ready for lunch?" Angel asked Ngozi with her eyes on Chance.

He turned his attention back to the bookshelves lining the wall.

"Yes, I already asked you to order lunch, remember? And is there something wrong with all the communication available between us...from your desk?" Ngozi asked, pointing her finger in that direction.

Angel smiled as she tucked a loose strand of her four bundles of waist-length weave behind her ear. She used to wear her hair in voluminous curls that gave her a hairdo like the Cowardly Lion from the *Wizard of Oz*. Ngozi had requested she wear it straight and pulled back into a ponytail while at work. Thankfully, she acquiesced.

"I also wanted to ask if you or your guest wanted somethin' to drink?" Angel asked, cutting her appreciating eyes on Chance again.

"No, thank you," Ngozi said politely, as she jerked her thumb hard a few times toward Angel's workstation.

With one last look at Chance's tall figure behind his back, Ngozi's young assistant reluctantly left them alone, but not before flicking her tongue at him in a move Ngozi knew had been a hit during her former profession. She added a long talk on not flirting with clients on the long mental list of things to school Angel on.

She closed the automated door.

Chance turned to eye it before focusing his attention on her. "She's...unexpected," he mused with a slight smile.

That she is.

Some of the partners were still not fully sold on her working there.

"No pictures," Chance observed, walking up to her desk.

"Too many reminders of death," she said truthfully, without thinking to censor herself.

"Death?" he asked.

"Nothing," she muttered, sitting back in her chair as she eyed him. "I'm sure you didn't set up a fake appointment with me just to survey my office."

Chance shook his head as he folded his frame into one of the chairs facing her desk. "Fake name. Real appointment. I would like you to represent me," he explained.

That surprised her, and her face showed it. She reached for a legal pad and one of her favorite extrafine-point pens filling a pink-tinted glass bowl on the corner of her desk. The firm had every technological advance available, but she preferred the feel of a pen on paper when assessing the facts of a new case. "Typically, I handle criminal cases," she began.

"I know," Chance said, smiling at her. "Congratulations on your win this morning."

"Thank you," she said graciously, wondering if his smile had the same effect on all women the way it did on her. "You saw the news?"

He nodded. "You looked beautiful, Ngozi."

Thump-thump-thump-thump-thump.

She fought for nonchalance as her heart pounded wildly, seeming to thump in her ears. "And smart," she added.

"Of course, but beautiful nonetheless, Ngozi."

Thump-thump-thump-thump-thump-thump-thump-thump-thump-thump.

She shifted her eyes away from his. "What type of trouble are you in?" she asked, seeking a diversion from her reaction to him.

"It's a civil matter," Chance told her, raising one leg to rest his ankle on the knee of the opposite one.

Ngozi set her pen down atop the pad. "I'm sure a man of your means already has proper representation for a civil case."

"I may be interested in moving all my business here to Vincent and Associates Law…if this case is successfully litigated," he said. "That's a revenue of seven figures, if you're wondering."

She had been.

Ngozi steepled her fingers as she studied him, trying her best to focus on the business at hand and not how the darkness of his low-cut hair and shadowy beard gave him an intense look that happened to be very sexy. The news of the Harvard grad and successful financier inventing a project management app and reportedly selling it for well over $600 million had taken the business and tech sectors by storm, but it was his backstory of claiming success in spite of his humble beginnings that made Ngozi respect his hustle. He retained a small percentage of ownership with the deal and served as a well-paid consultant on top, making several large investments beyond the sale of his app to only increase his wealth and holdings.

Chance Castillo was a man to be admired for his brains. He made smart money moves that even Cardi B could respect.

The senior partners would appreciate bringing his legal interests under the firm's umbrella, and it would take the assistance of other attorneys more equipped to handle matters outside her expertise…if she won the civil case.

"What is the case about?" she asked, her curiosity piqued as she reclaimed her pen from the pad.

Chance shifted his eyes to the window wall displaying the sun breaking through the heart of midtown Manhattan's towering buildings. "I'm sure you heard about the end of my engagement last year," he began.

Her eyes widened a bit at the hardness that suddenly filled the line of his jaw and his voice. Yes, she had heard. The story held almost as much prominence in the news as the sale of his app. Although she had avoided reading about gossip, it was hard to ignore as conversation filler at dinner parties and such.

"She was having an affair the entire time she planned a million-dollar wedding on my dime. The willingness to foot the bill was mine, I admit that," he said, shifting eyes that lacked the warmth and charm they'd once contained. "But doing so after she ends the engagement to be with another man, that I can't swallow. Not on top of the cost of the engagement ring, as well."

Ngozi paused in taking notes. "And the cost of the ring?"

"A million."

"Would you like that recouped, as well?"

"I wish I could recoup every cent I ever spent on her," he said, his voice cold and angry.

Ngozi tapped the top of her pen against the pad as she bit the corner of her mouth in thought. "You understand that gifts cannot be recovered."

He held up his hand. "That's why I said I *wish* and not I *want*. I understand those things are lost to me."

She nodded. "The name of your ex-fiancée?"

He frowned as if the very thought of her was offensive and distasteful. "Helena Guzman," he said, reaching into the inner pocket of his blazer to remove a folded sheet of paper to hand to her.

Ngozi accepted it and opened it, finding her contact information. She frowned a bit at her work address, recognizing it instantly. "She works for Kingston Law?"

"She's a real estate attorney," he said, rising to his feet and pushing his hands into the pockets of his jeans as he stood before the window. He chuckled. It was bitter. "I assume once she left her meal ticket behind, she put aside her plan to stop working."

He was angry. Still. It had been nine months or more.

She broke his heart.

Ngozi eyed his profile, feeling bad for him. Gone were the bravado and charm. This was a man dealing badly with heartbreak.

"Are you sure litigation is necessary?" she asked, rising from her desk to come around it.

"Yes."

She came to stand with him at the window, their reflection showing his stony expression and her glancing up at his profile. "Why the wait, Chance?"

He turned his head to look down at her, seemingly surprised by her sudden closeness. "I was out of the country," he answered, his eyes vacant.

This Chance was nothing like the man she'd met two weeks ago, or even the one he'd been when he first strolled into her office. Which was the facade?

She gave him a soft smile.

He blinked, and the heat in the depth of his eyes returned, warming her. "With you looking up at me, I could almost believe in—"

Thump-thump-thump-thump-thump.

"Believe in what?" she asked.

He shook his head, softly touched her chin and then turned his focus back to the view splayed out before them. "Will you take the case?" he asked.

Ngozi swallowed over a lump in her throat and put the distance back between them. "Is this about anger over her not marrying you—which is breach of promise to marry and is no longer a viable defense in certain states? Or do you feel you've been wronged and would like a cause of action for strictly financial remedy?"

Chance flexed his shoulders. "The latter" was his response.

Ngozi reclaimed her seat, not admitting that she

did not believe him. "I think a case of this nature is best presented before a jury. It will be a long way to go, particularly with Ms. Guzman being an attorney herself, but perhaps she will be willing to settle this out of court."

Chance nodded.

She made several notes on her pad before looking up at him again. "I will need the details of your relationship and its breakup, and any receipts and invoices you have pertaining to the purchase of the ring and the wedding should be provided."

He nodded once more.

"Chance," she called to him.

He looked at her.

Their eyes locked.

Thump-thump-thump-thump-thump.

"During the length of this case you are going to have to relive what was clearly a very difficult time for you," she said. "It may become fodder for the news—"

"Again," he injected.

"Right," she agreed. "I just want to be *sure* you want to pursue this."

He smiled at her. "I'm sure, Ngozi."

"And you're sure you want me to represent you?" she asked, ignoring the thrill of her name on his lips.

His smile widened. "I take any business or legal matters very seriously. Even the offer to move my interests to this firm was researched first. I joke and laugh a lot. I love life, I love to have fun, but I never play about my money."

She stood up and extended her hand. "Then let's get your money back, Mr. Castillo," she said with confidence.

He took her hand in his but did not shake it, instead raising it a bit to eye her body. "We should celebrate our future win with dinner and a night of dancing, *la tentadora*," he said.

Ngozi visibly shivered, even as she looked to her right through the glass wall of her office and, sure enough, discovered quite a few eyes on them, most widened in surprise and open curiosity. She jerked her hand away and reclaimed her seat as she cleared her throat. "Please make an appointment at the receptionist's desk for us to review the details of the case," she said, paying far too much attention to the notepad on her desk. "I will need that information to complete the summons."

Chance chuckled. "Was I just dismissed?" he asked.

"Yes," she said, glancing up at him with a smile.

"Hay más de una forma de atrapar al gato," he said, turning to walk out of her office with one last look back at her.

His words lingered with her long after he was gone, while she futilely tried to focus on her work.

There is more than one way to catch a cat.

It wasn't quite the proper saying, but nothing had been lost in translation.

Chance Castillo had made his intention very clear.

Ngozi put her chin in her hand and traced her

thumb across the same spot on her chin that he had touched.

Thump-thump-thump-thump-thump-thump.

She released a stream of breath through pursed lips.

This was uncharted territory...for the last year, at least.

This attraction. This reaction. This desire.

An awakening.

Ngozi swore as the all-too-familiar pings of guilt and regret nipped at her, seemingly an integral part of her DNA.

Her brother's death. Her parents' grief. Her husband's death.

She pushed aside her thoughts and focused on work, soon getting lost in the minutiae of motions, reviewing court minutes, and at the end of the day celebrating her latest win with a champagne toast from the senior partners.

That evening, behind the wheel of her caldera red Jaguar F-Type coupe, Ngozi put the five-liter V8 engine to good use once she was on I-80 West, headed to Passion Grove. The sky darkened as she passed the township's welcome sign. She was grateful for the panoramic roof as she made her way toward her parents' estate. She slowed to a stop and looked out into the distance at the town's heart-shaped lake. Soon the chill of winter would freeze it over and the townspeople would enjoy ice skating, but tonight the stars reflected against the gentle sway of the water and she found the serenity of it comforting.

Following an impulse, she parked the car on the street and then climbed out to swap her heels for the pair of running sneakers she kept in her trunk. With her key fob in her hand, Ngozi made her way up the street around the brick-paved path surrounding the lake. She took a seat on one of the wrought iron benches, crossing her legs and leaning forward to look out at the water.

Ngozi, come on. Come skate with me.

Ngozi smiled a bit, feeling as if she could see her late husband, Dennis, before her at the edge of the frozen lake, beckoning her with his arm outstretched toward her. It was not a dream, but a memory.

Christmas night.

Maxwell's "Pretty Wings" was playing via the outdoor surround system that streamed top pop hits around the lake during the winter.

Earlier, right after Christmas dinner, the lake had been crowded with townspeople enjoying snowball fights or ice skating, but now only a few remained as darkness claimed prominence and the temperature slid downward with the absence of the sun. Snow covered the ground, casting the night with an eerie bright glow as the moon and stars reflected down upon the sheen of the ice...

Ngozi had been happy just to watch Dennis effortlessly gliding upon the ice with the skill of an Olympian, but she slid on her ice skates and made her way to him, accepting his hands and stepping onto the ice. They took off together, picking up the speed they needed before gliding across the ice with Dennis in the lead and their hands clasped together.

When he tugged her closer, she yelled out a little until he held her securely in his arms, burying his head against her neck as she flung hers back and smiled up at the moon while they slid for a few dozen feet before easing to a stop...

A tear slid down her cheek, and she reached out as if to touch the all-too-vivid memory of better times.

Bzzzzzz.

She let her hand drop as the vibration of her phone brought her out of her reverie. Blinking and wiping away her tears with one hand, she dug her iPhone out of the pocket of her fitted blazer.

"Yes?" she answered.

"Ngozi?"

Her father.

She closed her eyes and fought to remove the sadness from her tone. "Hey, Dad," she said and then winced because it sounded too jovial and false to her ears.

"Hey, congrats on the win, baby girl," Horace said, the pride in his voice unmistakable. "I thought you would be home by now. You didn't say you had a meeting or event or anything."

Her interpretation of that: Why are you late?

She was as predictable as a broken clock being right at least two times out of the day. Predictable and perfunctory.

"I'm on the way," she said, delivering a half-truth.

"Good. Your mother had a council meeting and Reeds is serving up real food for us while she's gone."

Ngozi laughed. Her father disdained the vegan lifestyle as much as she did. "Steaks simmered in brown butter with mashed potatoes and two stiff bourbons on ice?" she asked as she rose to her feet and made the small trek back to her car, guided by the lampposts lining the street.

"Absolutely," he said with a deep chuckle. "Hurry!"

"On my way," she promised, turning and taking a few steps backward as she gave the lake one last look and released the memory.

Chapter 4

Two weeks later

Chance reached inside the jar of almonds he kept on his desk, gathering a few into his hand to toss into his mouth as he leaned back in the ergonomic chair. Since he'd hit his major windfall a couple of years ago and left behind his work in finance, he rarely used his home office, but for the last couple of days an idea for a new app had been nagging at him. So he took his morning run, returned to shower and then meditate, and then headed into his office to hammer out the details floating around in his head.

The normal blare of the music was gone. He needed quiet to focus, and his estate in Alpine provided him plenty of that.

Again, the app was a labor of necessity. Although he was no longer on an 8:00 a.m.–8:00 p.m. job, he still found a need to be productive. Unlike his wealthy friends who grew up with staff, Chance preferred to do without. Many were not aware that the staff seen during his lavish dinner parties were not full-time nor live-in. He used a household staffing agency on an as-needed basis.

But for someone who preferred solitude, yet also had an active social life, traveled frequently and at times conducted business on the go, to have a virtual personal or executive assistant was as good as the real thing—or with the right analytics and algorithms, even better.

Ding.

He glanced at the email notification on the screen. It was from Ngozi's firm. Another request for an appointment.

Chance ignored it with a chuckle as he rose from his chair and crossed the wide breadth of his office to leave it and enter the kitchen. He froze and frowned at the sight of his mother stirring a bowl at the island. She was so consumed with it that she didn't even notice him. He crossed his arms over his chest and leaned in the doorway before he cleared his throat.

Esmerelda looked up and smiled at the sight of him. "Hello, Chance. I thought you were sleeping," she said, moving about his kitchen with ease.

He released a heavy breath. He loved his mother. Adored her. He was so thankful for her contribution and sacrifice to his success. He loved to gift her whatever she wished for, except...

"Ma," he said, pushing off the doorjamb with his hand extended toward her. "Come on. Give it up."

Esmerelda stared at him.

He bent his fingers as he returned her stare.

She sucked air between her teeth and wiped her hands clean with a dish towel before reaching in her designer tote bag for her key ring. She mumbled things in Spanish as she worked one of the keys around the ring.

Chance didn't lower his arm until she came around the island and pressed the key against his palm with a jerk. "How many copies did you make?" he asked, sliding the key into the pocket of his cotton sleep pants. "This has to be the tenth key I have taken from you. It has to stop. One day you're gonna walk up in here and see *way* more of me and a lady guest than you want to."

Esmerelda waved her hand dismissively. "Nothing I haven't seen. I changed your diapers," she said, stirring a spatula in the large ceramic bowl again.

"Things are not the same," he balked.

"I hope not."

Chance shook his head, walking up to press his hands against the marble top of the island. "Ma, I *need* my privacy," he said, his voice serious.

Esmerelda avoided eye contact. "You need this stew," she stressed.

Bzzzzzz.

He reached for his cell phone from the pocket of

his sleep pants. Soon he smiled and then ignored the call from Ngozi's assistant.

Will you walk into my parlor? said the Spider to the Fly.

"How is your case coming?" Esmerelda asked.

"It's still in the early stages," he said, raising his arms above his head to stretch as he watched her.

"Have you heard from Ese Rubio Diablo?"

Chance shook his head. "And I don't want to," he said with honesty. "The time for talking is over."

Esmerelda nodded and glanced at him before she turned to set the bowl on the countertop next to the eight-burner Viking stove he rarely used. "It is no easy feat to overcome heartbreak," she said. "Nothing but time can do it. Time and…forgiveness, *mi amada*."

Chance had moved to the French door smart fridge for a bottle of water, but paused at her words and the softness of her tone. "You think I should forgive her and move on?" he asked in surprise.

Esmerelda turned from the stove. "In time, you will have to, for yourself if not for *that* witch," she said. "Trust me, I know."

He took a deep swig of the water before setting the bottle atop the island as he watched her. His mother was only in her late forties. Still young and beautiful, with an air and vibrancy that made her seem far younger than her years, but with a lifestyle of a woman twenty years her senior. As far as he knew, the only man in her life was his father, and that was a subject they rarely discussed. Yet it had not quelled his curiosity about the man he knew he favored in looks.

His mother had been just seventeen and fresh from a move to America from the Dominican Republic with her grandmother. She met and fell in love with Jeffrey Castillo, a young and handsome Afro-Cuban street dude whom she later found out to be more fabrication than truth and more lust than love. When she told him she was pregnant, he ended the relationship and began seeing another young woman who lived in the same Bronx apartment building as Esmerelda—something that caused her great pain and shame. In time, that relationship of his ended as well, and he soon moved out of their neighborhood. She never saw him again.

"¿Has perdonado a mi padre?" he asked of her forgiveness of his father, using Spanish to connect to the Latino heritage in them both—the mother he knew and the father he did not.

Esmerelda's face became bitter. "For breaking my heart? Yes," she said. "For breaking yours? *Never.*"

Chance came around the island to hug her petite frame to his side, pushing aside the pang of hurt he felt at the truth of her words. He'd never spoken of the hurt of not having a father in his life. The questions. The curiosity about him. The regrets. At times, the anger. "I'm good, Ma," he reassured her.

"You are better than good, *mi amada.*"

My beloved.

Bzzzzzz.

His phone vibrated atop the island. He moved away

from her to retrieve it as she turned back to the stove. Flipping it over, he looked down at the screen. *Jackpot*.

"I gotta take this," he said to his mother, picking up the phone and padding barefoot across the tiled floor back to his office. "Hello, Ngozi."

"Mr. Castillo, my staff has been attempting to reach out to you to set an appointment to come in and discuss the facts of the case you want to take to court," she stressed, her tone formal and indicating clear annoyance.

He held the phone to his ear with one hand and massaged his bare chest with the other as he stood at the windows behind his desk and looked out at his pool. "I apologize for that. My schedule has been hectic. In fact, I'm in the middle of something right now but I didn't want to miss your call."

"Chance," she said, in warning.

"Can we meet this evening? I know it's last-minute, but I will be flying out of the country later tonight—"

"Chance," she repeated slowly.

"Yes?" he asked.

"Where are you?"

He paused. *Should I lie? No, never lie.* "I'm home."

"Do you have the information I requested?"

"Yup," he said, eyeing the folder of information he'd had prepared for her the day after their first appointment.

"I'll be there by seven to pick it up."

Even better than his original plan to have her meet him at the airfield.

Click.

Whistling, he left his office and reentered the kitchen. "Ma, I appreciate the food," he said.

"No problem," she said. "I felt like some oxtails, and I like your kitchen better than mine."

"Do you want to have it remodeled?" he asked, always wanting to spoil her.

"No, Chance, it's a new house and I lied. I love my kitchen, but I love my son more," she stressed, giving him a stern eye to let him know she meant it.

"How long before you're done?" he asked with feigned nonchalance.

Esmerelda raised a brow and rolled her eyes. "A girl."

"A woman," he corrected with emphasis.

She shook her head. "You're kicking me to the curb for some noony-knack," she said, glancing back at him over her shoulder.

"I don't think sending you home to your four-bedroom French Tudor is kicking you to the curb," he drawled, crossing his strong arms over his chest.

"I could go get a mani-pedi at seven," she said.

"Throw in a massage and be gone by six," he bartered.

"Deal. No cash. I'll charge it," she assured him, patting her pocketbook.

"Same difference," he said.

He gave her a weekly allowance, paid her monthly utility bills and gave her an unlimited credit card—that she refused to use without his permission.

"I'm glad you're dating, Chance. You deserve to

be loved again," she said as she emptied a bowl of diced onions into a pan that soon sizzled.

He frowned deeply. "Love?" he scoffed. "No, I'm not looking for the lies of love again. You can forget about that. Helena taught me a lesson I will never forget. Trust no one. Nah."

Esmerelda pointed the tip of the spatula at him. "You're smarter than that. No one can live without love forever," she said.

"Says the woman who has only loved one man in her life," he rebutted.

Esmerelda looked at him as if he had suddenly grown a horn in the center of his handsome head. "Says the silly man who thinks his mama has only loved—or been loved—by one man in thirty years," she said, widening her eyes at him as she released a short laugh. "Silly Chance."

His mouth opened in shock.

"Just because you didn't see it, baby boy, don't mean it wasn't going down, o-*kay*?" she said, her Spanish accent thick. "I wasn't hot to trot, but I got *me*. O-*kay*? And that wasn't any of your business. O-*kay*?"

Chance frowned, shaking his head as if to clear it. "I'm done with this conversation," he said, tilting his head back to drain the last of the water in the bottle into his mouth.

"Yeah, I thought so." Esmerelda chuckled. "Ain't nothing dead on me."

"Let yourself out, Mama. Love you," he said over his shoulder as he left the kitchen.

"Bless his silly heart."

Chance pushed aside thoughts of his mother having a sex life and made his way through the massive house, then jogged up the stairs to his master suite. Standing before the walls of his closet, he admitted to feeling excited at seeing Ngozi again as he selected an outfit.

You deserve to be loved again.

He paused.

He desired Ngozi. He liked her spunk and cleverness. Being around her made him feel good.

But love wasn't in the equation.

Love—or what he thought was love—led to him being made a fool, and a public one at that.

"Nah, I'm good on that," he said to himself, selecting an outfit. "A brother's just trying to have fun with a beautiful lady. That's it. That's all."

Right?

"Right," he said, as if to reassure himself while he laid the clothes on his bed and made his way to his bathroom.

When he returned downstairs, fully dressed and subtly smelling of Creed Viking cologne, the scent of the stew permeated the lower level of the house. He headed to a large framed mirror on the wall beside the front doors, opening it to display the security monitors. He was scanning each room and both three-car garages to make sure his mother had taken leave when one of the monitors showed a red sports car pulling to a stop in front of the secured gate.

The driver's side window lowered, and Ngozi sat

behind the wheel with rose-gold aviator shades in place.

Chance smiled at the sight of her as she reached out and tapped the touch screen. *Just beautiful.*

His security system was automated, but he tapped the pad on its wall base anyway. "Come on in," he said, watching as the gate slid open, and soon she was on her way up the short driveway to him.

He closed the mirror front and then checked his appearance in it, smoothing his beard and adjusting the lightweight V-neck silk sweater he wore with linen slacks. He pushed the sleeves midway up onto his forearms before opening the door and walking down the steps to his stone-paved courtyard.

She parked at an angle before climbing from the car.

With his hands pushed into the pockets of his pants, he watched her, loving the way her hair was pulled back into a sleek ponytail that showed off her high cheekbones. The gray metallic sheath dress she wore fit her frame and complemented her shapely legs. The sun was just beginning to set, and the white uplight began to glow, casting a gleam against her deep brown complexion as she walked up to him. "Nice ride, Ms. Johns," he said. "You sure you can handle it?"

Ngozi slid her shades on top of her head as she glanced back at her vehicle and then looked up at him. "I'm not giving you an opening for a double entendre," she drawled.

He chuckled before giving her a smile. "Welcome to my home, Ngozi," he said.

"And a beautiful home it is," she said, looking around at the manicured lawn and the wrought iron accents on the French villa exterior.

"Would you like a tour?" he asked, surprised that her opinion mattered to him.

Ngozi crossed her arms over her small bosom and tapped one toe of her shoe against a stone paver. "Nope. I'm not falling for the banana in the tailpipe again, Eddie Murphy," she said. "Over the last two weeks, you have been elusive. I have suggested meetings in every *possible* location except my office."

Chance nodded.

"And yet, each and every time I have been unsuccessful," she said, undoing her arms and splaying her hands. "Do you have the paperwork and the timeline of your relationship—including its demise—with Helena Guzman?"

"Yes," he said, fighting hard not to smile because he knew her annoyance with him was genuine and understandable.

She clapped a few times and then clasped her hands together. "Thank you, Lord. Now...do you have it *here*?"

"Yes. It's in my office."

She arched a brow. *"Here?"* Ngozi stressed again. "Yes."

"Would have been so lovely if you had it in your hand to give to me right now, and send me on my way," she said.

He reached down for her hand, clasping it with his own before turning to walk up the steps. "What fun would that be?" he asked.

She followed him up the stairs and into the house, but when they stepped inside the grand foyer, she eased her hand from his. "Wow," she said, turning on her heels to look around at the elaborate metal chandelier and the towering height of the ceiling. "Nice."

He watched her as she walked up to the sculptures of the nude figures. He didn't miss when her mouth opened just a bit as she reached out to trace from one clavicle to the other on a few of the figures. Chance's gut clenched at the subtle and seemingly innocent gesture.

Damn.

"This is a lot of house," she said, glancing back at him as she withdrew her hand.

"Big house for a big man."

Their eyes met.

His heart pounded.

She looked away with a lick of her lips as if they were suddenly parched. "The…the paperwork," she reminded him gently, raising her hand to smooth the hair pulled up into her ponytail.

There were things Chance knew for sure, and other things he could only assume or guess—but his gut instinct rarely let him down. And there were two things he knew for sure over the time they'd spent together in the last two weeks. He desired Ngozi with an intensity that was distracting.

And Ngozi Johns wanted him just as badly.

The thought of striding up to her and pressing his lips against hers captured his attention at random moments throughout his day, and curiosity if her attitude in bed was as fierce as it was in court dominated his nights.

All of the telltale signs were there.

Long stares.

Little licks of her lips.

Catching her watching him.

Hunger in her eyes.

Moments where the will to resist him was seemingly weak.

But each time, she fought and won over her desire for him, leaving him disappointed and craving her even more.

But this chess game of desire between them was always her play. Her move. Her time.

Releasing a short breath that did nothing to quell the racing of his pulse, Chance pointed beyond the wrought iron stairs. "This way," he said, clearing his throat and leading the way into the chef's kitchen.

"Whatever that is smells so good," she said, eyeing the stove as they passed the massive island. "Kudos to your chef."

"My mom made oxtail stew," he said, opening the door to the office and turning on the ceiling light.

"You live with your mom?" she asked from behind him.

Chance picked up the folder and looked at her in disbelief. "I am a grown-ass man," he said as he handed it to her. "I live alone."

She held up her hand as if to say *my bad* before taking it from him and flipping through it. "I have people on staff and couriers on call to pick up stuff like this, Mr. Castillo," she said, chastising him.

He leaned against the edge of his desk, crossing his legs at the ankles. "I enjoy your company, Ms. Johns," he countered smoothly. Honestly.

Again, their eyes met.

That vibe between them pulsed, electrifying the air.

"I don't mix business and pleasure, Chance, not with clients nor coworkers," she said.

He wasn't sure if she was schooling him or reminding herself about the line she had drawn in the sand.

He eyed her, finding himself unable to stop. His eyes dropped to her mouth.

"Show me your beautiful house," Ngozi offered, turning from him to leave the office.

Her invitation to remain in his company both surprised and pleased him.

"You think I can get a to-go box of some of your mama's stew?" she asked with a coquettish smile that brightened her eyes.

"Or you could stay and have dinner with me," he offered, coming to a stop before where she leaned back against the island.

Ngozi swallowed hard as she looked up at him. "Chance," she whispered softly, her eyes dropping to his mouth as she licked the corners of her own. "Come on, help me out."

He put his hands on either side of her, leaning toward her, feeling drawn into her as he inhaled the warm scent of her perfume in the small and intimate space between them. "Help you what?"

He saw her tremble. It made him weak. That attraction—an *awareness*—throbbed between them. It was hard to resist. Passion. Chemistry. Electricity.

"Fight this," she implored, her eyes soft and filling with the heat rising in her.

"Nah," he drawled slowly and low in his throat as he lowered his head and pressed a soft kiss to the corner of her mouth.

It was softness. Sweetness.

"Chance," she sighed with just a little hint of aching in her tone.

He shook his head as he smiled and then pressed his lips against hers.

The tip of her clever tongue darted out to lick at the little dip in the center of his bottom lip.

He grunted in hot pleasure, feeling his entire body jolt with an unseen surge, a current. This power created by a connection between them had been stoked over the last two weeks, taunting and tempting them with a force that could not be ignored.

There was no woman he'd ever wanted so much in his life.

When she brought her quivering hands up to clutch at the front of his sweater, he followed her lead—her unspoken acceptance—and gripped her hips to pull their bodies close together as they deepened the kiss and gave in to the passion that could not be denied.

It started out slow, as if they were trying to savor every moment.

Chance brought his hands up to her back, massaging the small of it as he drew the tip of her tongue into his mouth and suckled it. She whimpered as she brought her hands up to hold the sides of his face.

He felt her hunger and matched it with his own, relinquishing control as he gently broke their kiss to press his mouth to her neck. He inhaled deeply of the warm scent of her perfume, and he enjoyed the feel of her racing pulse against his lips. And when he suckled that spot, she gasped and flung her head back.

"Yes," she whispered hotly, her hands rising from his cheeks to the back of his head to press him closer.

Chance felt a wildness stir in him as he suckled her deeply, not caring if he left a mark as he brought his hands down to pull her body from the edge of the island and glide his hands to her buttocks. Cupping them. Massaging the softness. Loving the feel of his hardness pressed against her stomach as he ached for her.

"Ngozi," he moaned against her neck, feeling lost in her. Her scent. Her presence. Her vibe. Her energy.

Her being. Her everything.

He grabbed her by the waist and hoisted her up on top of the island as he undid the zipper on the back of her dress. Eased the top of her dress down, moved back to take in the sight of her small but plump breasts in the black strapless lace bra she wore before he quickly jerked off his sweater and flung it away.

Chance stood there between her open thighs with

the skirt of her dress up around the top of her thighs, eyeing her. The hint of her lace bikini panties peeked out between her legs, with her chest slightly heaving as her hard nipples pressed against the barely there lace, her eyes glazed and the gloss on her swollen lips smudged from his kisses. He had never seen anything sexier.

Ngozi Johns was allure personified.

And when her eyes took in the sight of his chest and abs, and moved down to his hard curve tenting his linen pants, he saw both her appreciation and anticipation. Never had he wanted so much to live up to expectations.

One small move forward and she was back in his arms, her flesh against his as she wrapped her arms around his neck when their lips met again with one kiss and then a dozen more. Small but satisfying, and leading to more as he offered her his tongue and she touched it with her own with a hungry moan.

The sound of one shoe and then another hitting the floor echoed in the moments before Ngozi wrapped her legs around his waist. The heel of her foot dug into his buttock, and Chance couldn't care less. He kissed a trail down her body until he lightly bit the edge of her bra to jerk it down below one breast with his teeth. The first stroke of his tongue against her nipple caused Ngozi to arch her back.

"Yessss," she cried out. "Yes. Yes. Yes."

He sucked harder. Deeper. Pulling as much of her breast into his mouth as he could.

Ngozi reached down between them and began to undo his belt with rushed movements.

Chance stepped up onto the foot rail lining the island to make the job easier for her. And when she pressed her mouth to the hard ridge between his biceps, it was his turn to tremble. She kissed a trail to one hard nipple to circle it with her tongue.

That move surprised him, and the moan of pleasure he released came from his gut.

She guided her lips to the other, and this time she sucked that nipple into her mouth before lightly grazing it with her teeth as his loose-fitting pants fell down around his ankles.

He was so anxious for her that he could hardly think straight. His lengthy manhood was so hard that his loins ached to be surrounded by her, deeply stroking until satisfied. He removed his boxers, freeing his thick curving member. It lay atop the island between her open thighs, the coolness of the marble surprisingly arousing to him.

"Oh...oh my." She sighed in pleasure as she looked down at his inches and then up at his eyes.

"Look," he said, gesturing downward with his head.

She did.

With no hands, he raised it off the cool marble and brought it back down upon it with a light thud.

Her jaw slowly dropped. "You...uh...you really have great control of that," she said.

"Imagine when I use my hips," he forewarned with a sultry chuckle.

Ngozi licked her lips and swallowed hard. "Why imagine?" she asked, sliding backward along the smooth marble until she was in the center of it. She lay back, her eyes on him as she slid her pinkies inside the edge of her lace bikini panties and raised her buttocks to ease them down until they lay in a pile by her feet.

Chance quickly retrieved protection for them from his wallet and sheathed himself with it before he climbed atop the island with her, his erection leading between her open legs. As soon as he lay on top of her, her hands were on his back and then his buttocks, gripping his firm cheeks as he arched his hips and guided his hardness inside her with one firm thrust.

He looked down into her face as her eyes widened, and she gasped before she released a tiny little wail and arched her back. He could feel her walls throbbing against his hard length. He buried his face against the side of hers as his body went tense. "You're so tight, Ngozi," he said near her ear, the strain in his voice clear.

"I feel you. I... I... I feel it," she whispered with a breath. "I needed this. I *needed* this."

Her words seemed like a revelation to herself... and they were pure motivation to him.

Chance was more than ready to give her *exactly* what she needed.

He eased his hands beneath her buttocks and raised her hips up a bit as he began to stroke inside her, seeking and finding her mouth to kiss her.

"Yes, yes, yes," she panted in between kisses with an urgency.

He felt her body against him. Wet. Hot. Throbbing. Her moans of passion were a catalyst. Her hands switched between gripping or massaging his back and buttocks, pushing him closer and closer to the edge of his climax. But he was not ready for the ride to end, and so he would pause in his strokes many times as it eased.

"We're moving," she said.

He raised his head from where he was biting down on her shoulder and saw that each of his thrusts had propelled their bodies down the length of the slippery island. A few more inches and her head would be over the side. He looked down at her, and they shared a smile. "I want to make you come, not give you a concussion."

Her eyes warmed over before she lifted her head and licked hotly at his mouth as she raised her arms high above her head and gripped the edge of the island tightly. The move caused her breasts to spread and her nipples to point to the ceiling, drawing his eyes. He shifted his body to pull one and then the other with his mouth.

"Mmm," she moaned, arching her back again.

He looked up at her. "Still want it?" he asked, his voice deep.

She matched his look with dazed eyes. "Still *need* it," she stressed, working her hips so that her core glided down the length of his hardness.

Chance crushed his mouth down upon hers as he

drove his maleness in to fill her again and again and again. His pace quickened. His erection hardened. His thrusts deepened.

Her cries of wild abandon fueled him.

The sight of her breasts lunging back and forth with each hard thrust or circular motion of his hips excited him.

And the feel of her walls tightening down on him with white-hot spasms of her own release pushed him over the edge. He willingly fell into the abyss, tumbling into pleasure and excitement that blinded him to everything but the feel of her body and the look of surprise and rapture on her face.

And when he saw that tears filled her eyes as she trembled, he kissed them away and held her tightly, turning them over so that her body was now atop his and her head was nuzzled against his chest. He could feel her heart pounding as hard and as fast as his own. He looked up to the towering custom coffered ceiling as he waited for his equilibrium to return.

"I... I...have to go."

Chance jerked his head up as Ngozi rushed to rise, standing up on the island and then stepping over his legs to climb down off it. Not even the delectable sight of her bare bottom could distract him from the sudden shift in mood. "Hey, Ngozi, what's wrong?" he asked, quickly jumping down to grab a wad of paper towels from the countertop holder.

She jerked her strapless bra up over her breasts and fixed her dress so that she wore it properly but leaving the back unzipped. "This was a mistake," she said.

Oh hell.

He removed his condom inside the towels as he watched her frantically gather her discarded panties into a wad in her hand. "Ngozi," he said again, reaching for her arm as she struggled to step into her heels.

"Just let me leave, Chance," she pleaded, jerking out of his grasp and bending down to grab both shoes by the heels with one hand instead.

"What the hell happened?" he asked, confused by her behavior.

"Bye, Chance," she said, turning away with an awkward wave to leave the kitchen.

Naked and uncaring, he followed behind her. "Ngozi, at least put your damn shoes on," he said.

She stopped in the foyer, looking back at him. Her eyes darted down to his now-limp member, and she whirled away from him to hold the edge of the table as she slid on each of her shoes.

"Not exactly sure how you go from *I need this* to needing to get the hell away from me," he said.

She continued on to the door, her perfect ponytail now mussed and her makeup smeared. She opened the door and paused. "It was amazing, Chance, but a mistake," she said, not turning to face him. "You're my client. You *were* my client. I can't represent you now—"

Chance scowled. "So not only are you making me feel bad for giving you exactly what you said you needed, but you also won't rep me anymore. You know what? Unnecessary drama, Ngozi. Just…unnecessary. If that's how you want it, then fine."

She turned. "You got what you wanted, right?" she asked.

No, I got more than I asked for.

"Whatever you say," Chance said, turning to walk away.

When the front door closed, he paused, wiping his bearded chin with his hand as he shook his head. *Damn.*

Chapter 5

"You're so tight, Ngozi."

"I feel you. I... I... I feel it. I needed this. I needed *this."*

Ngozi shivered at the hot memory and then was flooded with embarrassment, raising her hands to press her palms against her cheeks. She had begged the man to please her. Making love with Chance atop that island had been so out of character for her. Not Miss Prim-and-Proper. Not Miss Perfect.

But...

It had felt so right. So good. So *necessary.*

But that didn't take away from her unprofessionalism. She had broken her one rule of not mixing business with pleasure. For that, she was disappointed in herself and ashamed.

But…

At odd moments through the last few days and each night, she had thought of him, inside her, riding her, pleasing her…and she wanted more.

"Whoo," she sighed, releasing a shaky breath as she leaned back in her chair in her office at VAL and closed her eyes, hoping to abate the steady throb of her femininity and the hardening of her nipples as her arousal came in a rush at the very *thought* of Chance Castillo and every delicious, long, curving inch—

"Mmm."

She popped up out of her chair, her eyes wide, and pressed the back of her hand to her lips, surprised by her own moan of pleasure. She looked out the glass wall of her office and was happy no one had noticed her startled reaction. She smoothed the fitted black lambskin dress with embroidered pocket she wore before reclaiming her seat with a shake of her head.

"Come on, Ngozi. Gather yourself," she said, reaching for her conference phone to hit the button for the speakerphone before she dialed an extension.

"Yes, Ms. Johns?"

"Hello, Roberta. Can Larry take a quick call?" she asked the legal secretary of Larry Rawlings.

"Sure thing. Hold on, I'll transfer you in."

Beep.

He was on the line within a second. "Yes, Ngozi?"

"Hey, Larry, I just wondered if Mr. Castillo followed up with you," she said, shifting her gaze out at the sun beginning to set beyond the towering Manhattan buildings.

"Yes, he did. Matter of fact, a messenger just dropped off a folder of receipts with a detailed outline of dates," he said. "We have an appointment to meet next to get the ball rolling."

In her haste to leave Chance's home she had left the folder of information behind.

"Good," she said, confused by her disappointment. "Thanks for picking up the ball for me, but I know you will get the job done, and hopefully the firm will be able to cover some other interests for Mr. Castillo, as well."

"I'm on it."

"Thanks, Larry. Enjoy your weekend."

She ended the call.

Chance had moved on. There had been no calls or attempts to finagle more of her time. There was no more chasing to be done.

Ngozi winced as she thought of his annoyance at her. She could understand.

So not only are you making me feel bad for giving you exactly what you said you needed, but you also won't rep me anymore.

Glancing at her watch, she rose and retrieved her black wool and lambskin belted jacket from her closet before grabbing her clutch and portfolio, as well. She quickly began packing files into the crocodile briefcase.

"Good night, Ms. J."

She glanced up at Angel with a smile. "Have a good weekend," she bid her assistant, before returning to her task. Suddenly, she looked up. "Not *too* good. You're on probation."

"Yes, I know. You remind me *every* weekend," she said. "What do you have planned? Any fun?"

Ngozi looked taken aback. "I have fun, Angel," she said.

Three days ago, I had plenty of it atop an island in the middle of a kitchen.

Her personal assistant looked disbelieving.

"As a matter of fact, tonight I am attending a charity dinner and I'm looking forward to it," she lied.

Alek and Alessandra had purchased a few tables in support of a charity benefiting inner-city youth. The odds were in favor of Chance being in attendance, as well. Their seeing each other was inevitable. They shared a godchild and friends.

What if he brought a date?

Ngozi came out from around her desk. "I am headed home to find just the *right* outfit," she said as they walked down the length of the office together to the elevator.

Chance stood at the entrance of the open brass door leading into the grand ballroom of midtown Manhattan's Gotham Hall and took in the sight of the elegant decor with bluish lighting that highlighted the gilded ceiling with its stained glass center and the oval-shaped room's marble flooring. It was as beautiful as every other gala event. Tables set. Flower arrangements centered. Candles lit. Music playing.

Gourmet food ready to be served. Drinks prepped to be poured. Attendees mingling in their finery.

He was bored.

He was better with writing the check and wishing the charity well, and didn't need the pomp and circumstance surrounding it. It all was a bit much for the boy from the wrong side of the tracks, but alas, he had long since learned to play the role. To show up. Write the check. Rub shoulders. Advance.

And then find his fun elsewhere.

He spotted Alek at the large bar and made his way toward him, weaving his way through the crowd of people filling the large room. "Good to see familiar faces," he said.

Alek turned, and they shared a handshake.

"Right," Alek said. "Thanks for coming. I know this is not your thing. Why'd you change your mind?"

Chance shrugged before leaning against the bar and looking about the room.

"No date?"

At that moment, Chance spotted Ngozi as she stepped into the open doorway of the ballroom. His heart instantly pounded at the sight of her in the floor-length illusion gown with a fringe skirt and plunging neckline lined with lace scalloped edges that made her décolletage all the more appealing. *Damn.*

Memories of nuzzling his face in that soft spot between her breasts as he made love to her came in a rush. Flashes of hot moments they shared in his kitchen replayed—the same memories that had plagued him since that evening. In that moment, she brushed her sleek hair back from her face and entered the ballroom. Any hints of the anger he once held for her faded like a fine mist.

He missed her.

He wanted her.

And it took every bit of strength contained within him not to call her. To accept that the heated moments they shared had been a mistake, just as she had said.

He didn't believe that. The energy and excitement he felt in her presence was like nothing he had ever experienced with any other woman. Not even Helena.

And the sex?

His gut clenched.

He thought he'd gone mad in those furious moments as he climaxed inside her.

His eyes were on her as she made her way across the room. He watched as she reached the table. Alessandra rose to greet her, and the two women hugged each other, exchanged words and shared a laugh.

Alek turned and pushed a double shot of tequila into Chance's hand.

"Huh?" he said, looking down at the drink in surprise before taking it from his friend.

"There's Ngozi," Alek said, sipping from his drink with one hand and holding a flute of champagne with the other. "Wow, that dress is unforgettable. I wonder who she's trying to tempt tonight."

"Me," Chance answered, looking on as both Ngozi and Alessandra looked across the room toward them.

"Huh?" Alek said, frowning. "Am I missing something?"

"Plenty," Chance said before taking a deep sip of his drink.

"Care to fill me in?"

"Nope."

"Cool," Alek said, motioning for the bartender. "Another flute of Dom, please."

With drinks in hand, Chance eyed how the blue lights reflected so perfectly against her dark complexion and highlighted her back in the low cut of the dress. "Why is she so damn fine?" he asked, accepting that his nerves would forever be shot in her presence as he neared her.

"I couldn't answer that because I got a hella fine one my damn self," Alek said, giving his wife an appreciative eye in the strapless white dress she wore with a large statement necklace of gold.

"Hello, Ngozi," he said.

She turned and looked up at him. "Chance. How are you?" she asked, accepting the flute he handed to her.

Their hands lightly grazed each other, and their eyes locked.

And there it was again. Big. Bold. Undeniable. Constant.

Chemistry.

Ngozi barely heard the live band's rendition of Minnie Riperton's "Loving You" as she tried her best not to stare at Chance, but they both seemed to be failing at it. She would look at him, he would look away. She would feel his eyes on her, like heat, but when she glanced in his direction, his attention was elsewhere.

Several times she caught both Alek's and Alessandra's eyes shifting back and forth between them. Her heart was pounding so rapidly that she feared it would outpace her and send her into a total blackout. And when Chance rose, tossing his linen napkin on his untouched food, and came around the table to extend his hand to her, she pursed her glossy lips and released a breath filled with all her nervous anxiety.

She looked up at him, down at his big beautiful hand, and then back up at his face, knowing that sliding her hand in his was much more than an invitation to dance.

"Come on," he mouthed.

She couldn't resist.

"What am I missing?" she heard Alessandra ask from behind her.

"Hush, baby," Alek suggested.

Ngozi hung her beaded egg-shaped clutch around her wrist and accepted Chance's offer. Her hand was warm where they touched as he led her onto the dance floor beneath the oscillating lights. He stopped and gently tugged her to pull her body close to his. She settled her arms across his back as he settled his around her waist. The top of her head came to his chin, and as they danced, their bodies seemed to fit. To work. To click. Like lock to key.

He dipped his head. "Still don't need me anymore?" he asked near her ear.

She leaned back to look up at him. "Chance," she whispered, her resolve sounding feeble to her own ears.

"I came here tonight looking for you," he admitted.

"Really?" she asked, acutely aware of how warm his hand was against her bared lower back.

"And you wore this dress tonight for me, *la tentadora*. Right?"

The temptress.

Yes, her dress fit that bill.

She looked away from him and licked the corner of her mouth. "In case you brought a date," she confessed, arching her brow as she tilted her head to look up at him once again.

He chuckled. It was deep and rich.

"Your hand feels good rubbing my neck."

Ngozi lowered her hand to his back once more, not even realizing she had been stroking his nape with her fingertips. It felt natural showing affection toward him.

He held her arm high in the air and slowly danced around her before pulling her back into his embrace and then spinning her out and reeling her back in to him. "You should smile more often, Ngozi Johns," he said.

"I haven't had much to smile about in a really long time," she admitted, surprised by her candor.

"Me either," Chance said. "So let's have fun together. Nothing serious. No ties. Just fun."

Why does that sound so good to me?

"Your caveat about not dating clients no longer fits, because you no longer represent me," he reminded her.

That's true.

"I don't know, Chance," she said, allowing herself to stroke his nape again.

"Okay, think about it, but let me offer this?" he began, trailing his finger up her spine.

Ngozi shivered and her nipples hardened as all of her pulse points throbbed—including the now-swollen bud nestled between the lips of her core. "What?" she whispered, her eyes falling to his soft mouth.

"Let's have fun tonight and worry about tomorrow when it comes."

Ngozi always put what was right before what she wanted. Always. With her parents. With her marriage. With her career.

Sometimes being so damn perfect was so damn tiring.

"I need it," he moaned near her ear, his breath lightly breezing against the lobe.

She feigned indignation. "Really, you're playing the need card?"

"You played it first. Remember?"

"I haven't been able to forget."

They shared a laugh that was all too knowing.

"It was *fun*," Ngozi acknowledged, her body trembling.

"Damn right it was."

"Let's go," she said, stepping back from him.

"We're gone," Chance agreed, grabbing her hand as they made a hasty retreat toward the door.

Ngozi sat up on the bed and ran her hand through her tousled hair as she looked down at Chance's nude body sprawled out beside her. The contours of his body were defined by the silver moonlight through the open curtains of the hotel suite's balcony doors. The soft buzz of his snores was thankfully muffled by the pillows over his head.

He deserves his rest.

She shook her head in wonder at his skill as she reached for her iPhone on the bedside table. She held the lightweight cover across the front of her body as she rose from the bed gently and stepped over her $3,000 gown carelessly left on the floor in their haste. As she made her way to the open balcony doors, she dialed her parents' landline phone number, tapping the tip of her nail against the rose-gold sequin as it rang.

"Hello."

"Hey, Reeds," she said, hating that she felt like a high schooler sneaking out for the night.

I am a successful over-thirty-years-old attorney—

"Is everything okay?" the house manager asked, his voice filled with concern.

"Everything's fine, Reeds. Everything okay there?" she asked, looking out at the moon shining down on the New York skyline.

"Same as always. Your parents already turned in for the night."

"Thank God. I thought they would wait up for me."

"They asked me to do it," Reeds admitted with a chuckle. "No one is roaming about this time of night but me and one of your father's Cuban cigars."

"Enjoy your cigar and go to bed," Ngozi said. "I'm staying in the city tonight."

"Okay. Be safe. Good night, Ngozi."

"Night," she said softly, hating the relief she felt that she had dodged talking to either of her parents.

"Should I be jealous?"

Ngozi whirled, causing the blanket to twist around her legs as she eyed Chance rising from the bed to walk over to her. She ran her hand through her hair, failing to free it of the tangles created during their love play. "No," she said, looking up at him as he stood before her, naked and beautiful in the moonlight. "Because this is only for the night. Remember?"

"Give me the weekend," Chance requested. "We can fly wherever you want in the world. Name it. It's yours."

Ngozi shook her head, lightly touching her kiss-swollen lips with her fingertips. "I can't."

He bent his strong legs and wrapped his arms around her waist to heft her up. She had to look down into his upturned face, and gave in to the urge to stroke his cheek. "Paris. Dubai. Italy," he offered. "Ibiza, Antigua, French Riviera, Bora Bora…"

Chance paused and smiled.

"Your life is different from mine, huh?" she asked.

He bent his head to press a kiss to her clavicle, then drew a circle there with his tongue.

Ngozi let her head fall back, the ends of her weaved tresses tickling the small of her back. "I haven't had a break in a long while," she admitted with a sigh. "And I do carry my passport in my wallet."

Chance carried her over to lay her on the bed, and then grabbed the blanket to pull off her body and fling onto the floor.

Feeling flirty, she rolled over onto her stomach and glanced back at him over her shoulder as she raised her buttocks. Her smile spread as he became erect before her eyes. *He really is all kinds of perfection.*

Chance lightly held her ankles and slid her body across the bed until she was bent over it. He reached onto the bedside table for one of the dozen foil packets of condoms. She watched him roll the ribbed latex down his length before she closed her eyes and sighed in pleasure. The warmth of his body radiated as he knelt behind her and curved his body against hers as he licked a hot trail up her spine and then lightly bit her shoulder. And when he spread her open and guided every inch of his hardness inside her, she grimaced and clutched the sheet in her fist as her body tried to conform to the fit and hard feel of him.

"Chance?" she said, looking back at him as he stroked inside her, slowly enough for her to take note of each inch as it went in and out of her.

"Yeah, baby," he said, looking down at the connection before tilting his head to the side to give her his attention.

"Not so deep," she said, closing her eyes. "I don't need all of it. I'm good."

He chuckled a little as he pulled out some. "Better?" he asked, biting the side of his tongue.

She relaxed her body with an eager nod.

He slid his hand around her body and pressed his fingertips against her moist and swollen bud, gently stroking it as he thrust inside her.

Ngozi's eyes and mouth widened.

"I thought making you come a couple times make up for it," he said thickly.

"A couple?" she asked with a lick of her lips.

"Oh *yes*," he stressed.

"Oh my."

She chose Italy.

Chance eyed Ngozi standing there on the balcony of the sprawling villa he rented in Sorrento off the Amalfi Coast. Her arms were splayed as she gripped the railing of the private balcony off their palatial bedroom as she overlooked the gardens, the grass-covered mountains and the nearby bluish-green waters of the Mediterranean Sea. Her hair was loose, and she wore a red strapless maxi dress that clung to her body when the wind blew.

He found her so breathtaking that he paused his steps as his pulse raced and his heart pounded.

She turned and smiled at him at the exact moment that the sunlight framed her from behind, bringing to mind dark chocolate lightly dusted with gold powder.

Ngozi Johns was trouble.

Forcing a smile, he continued over to her, handing her the goblet of white wine he carried. "A little fun isn't so bad, right?" he asked, leaning back against the railing as he sipped from his snifter of tequila.

"Yes, but too much is not for the best either," she countered.

"Here's to balance," he said, raising his snifter.

"To balance," she agreed, touching her glass to his.

Chance looked beyond her to the downtown area

of Sorrento in the far distance. "I still can't believe you agreed to stay through Monday," he said.

"I can't believe you made it worth the extra work I will have on Tuesday to catch up with my crazy workload," Ngozi said, moving away from him to lie on one of the lounges.

He watched her drape her hair over one shoulder before extending one leg and bending the other as she closed her eyes and let the sun toast her flawless skin a deeper shade of brown.

From the moment they had arrived in Italy on his jet, they had squeezed in as much sightseeing, fine foods and fun as they could during the days, and fell into that heated abyss they created throughout the nights. They were scheduled to leave tomorrow afternoon, and for him it was a mixed blessing.

He didn't trust how she made him feel.

The stain Helena had left on his life and his belief in his instincts was ever present.

"Can I ask you something?" he called over to her, seeking refuge from his thoughts.

Ngozi waved her bent leg back and forth as she looked over at him. "I'm a lawyer. Questions are my life," she said.

Chance took a sip of his drink, looking at her over the rim of the crystal as he closed the short distance between them to sit on the lounge beside her. "The first time, in my kitchen, why did you run away like that?" he asked. "We were both lying there caught up in a *damn* good moment, and it made you run?"

She reached for her wine and took a deep sip as if stalling for time or gathering courage.

He said nothing, patiently waiting for an answer to a question that had remained with him since the moment she fled.

"In that *damn* good moment," she began, not meeting his eyes, "I felt guilty that the first time I ever climaxed in my life was with someone other than my husband."

First time?

"It felt like a betrayal," she continued. "It felt like that *damn* good moment overshadowed my entire sex life with him. So, it was glorious and shocking and damn good and…hurtful."

"And now?" he asked, not really sure what to say.

Ngozi leveled her eyes on him. "Still damn good," she admitted with a smile, sliding her leg onto his lap.

"Still hurtful?" Chance asked as he turned to straddle the lounge chair facing her. He ran his hands up the smooth expanse of her legs, from her ankles to the V at the top of her thighs.

"I'm getting better with it," she said softly, her chest rising and falling.

He took note of her reaction to him and tossed the edge of her dress up around her hips, exposing her clean-shaven mound and her core to him. "And are you satisfied?" he asked, bending to bless each of her soft thighs with a kiss.

He felt her tremble as she softly grunted in pleasure.

"Each and *every* time," Ngozi confessed, setting her wineglass down before she reached over to smooth one hand over the back of his head.

"Then let me go for a perfect record," he said, his words breezing against her core in the seconds before he suckled her clit into his mouth.

Ngozi descended the stairs from Chance's jet, giving him a smile of thanks when he extended his hand to help her down off the last step. Hand in hand, they walked across the tarmac to the two black-on-black SUVs awaiting their arrival.

The extended weekend was over.

She could hardly believe the whirlwind of it. The shopping for clothes and undergarments, the long flight to Italy, the sightseeing, the delicacies, the lovemaking and so much more. It seemed like much longer than three days.

It was over, just as they had agreed.

At the first SUV, she turned and faced him. "Thank you for the escape. Thank you for giving me what I didn't know I needed, Chance Castillo," she said.

"Same here."

His eyes dipped to her lips.

She licked them.

"Can we say goodbye to what we shared with a kiss?" he asked.

She stepped toward him and rose up on the tip of her toes to cover his mouth with her own.

He moaned as he wrapped a strong arm around

her waist, picking her up to level their mouths as he deepened the kiss.

With regret, and a few soft touches of their lips, Chance and Ngozi ended it, both stepping away.

With one last look at him, she turned and allowed the driver to open the rear door so that she could climb onto the leather seat. With one last wave, she faced forward and was proud of herself for not looking back as the driver closed the door and drove the vehicle away.

Chance's mansion was quiet and dimly lit. He found the setting necessary as he struggled with his thoughts. From the time he was a poor kid with wealthy classmates up until the moment he sold his app, he had always relied on his guts. That all changed when the woman he thought loved him revealed her betrayal.

The last thing he wanted was another relationship. Another opportunity to be burned and betrayed. Embarrassed. Disrespected.

But I miss her already. I miss Ngozi.

He wasn't ready to pretend that nothing had happened between them. With her, there had been no thoughts of Helena and the havoc she'd wrought on his life. With Ngozi, he had felt lighthearted again. He'd had fun.

Security check. Front exterior gate.

At his alarm system sending out an alert, Chance picked up the tablet on the sofa where he sat in the den. He checked the surveillance video. At the sight of the car sitting there, he squinted even as he tapped the screen to unlock the gate.

Dropping the tablet back onto the couch, he rose and made his way across the expansive house to the grand foyer. He pulled one of the front double doors open and stood in the entrance as he watched her climb from her car and walk over to the front steps to look up at him.

"I thought maybe for a little while longer, we could have some more fun together," Ngozi said, climbing the steps to lightly trace the ridged grooves of his abdomen with her finger.

Without a word, Chance captured her hand in his and turned to walk back inside his home with Ngozi close behind him.

Chapter 6

Two months later

"Hello, Aliyah," Ngozi cooed to her goddaughter as she held her in her arms where she sat on one of the chaise longues in her nursery.

Alessandra sat in the other, smiling as she looked on at her friend and her baby daughter. "You ready for one of those?" she asked.

Ngozi gave her a side-eye. "No, I am not," she stressed, moments before she bent her head to press her face in the baby's neck to inhale her scent.

"Lies," Alessandra drawled with a chuckle.

Ngozi shrugged one shoulder before shifting the baby upward to rest against her belly. "Okay, maybe one day, but not now."

"And not Chance?"

Ngozi frowned in confusion. "What about Chance?"

"What exactly is going on with you two?" Alessandra asked.

A hot memory of her biting down into the softness of a pillow with her buttocks high in the air as he gripped her fleshy cheeks and stroked deep inside her from behind played in Ngozi's mind.

Her cheeks warmed and the bud between her legs throbbed to life.

"Just fun. Nothing serious," she said.

But I miss him even right now.

"I figured that when you two spent Thanksgiving and Christmas apart."

Truth? She had thought of him on both holidays, and their texting had not sufficed to slay her longing for him.

"And there won't be any kissing at midnight on New Year's Eve either," Ngozi said. "Neither one of us are looking for anything more than what we have, which is nice *private* fun to pass the time."

More truth? He had become a new normal in Ngozi's life.

Ding-ding.

As a notification rang out, Ngozi picked up her iPhone from the lounge to read her text. She smiled as her heart raced. *Chance.*

He'd spent the holidays with his mother and family in Cabrera.

Chance: Coming home 2night. Can I see u?

Yessss, she thought.

"Pass the time until what?" Alessandra asked.

"Huh?" Ngozi asked, pausing in answering his text with one of her own.

Alessandra arched a brow and looked pointedly down at her friend's iPhone. "You and Chance are passing the time until what?" she asked again.

Ding-ding.

"Until it's not fun anymore," Ngozi said as she opened his text.

Chance: I can send a car.

Aliyah began to stir and cry in her arms.

"It's time for her to eat," Alessandra said, rising to walk across the large room to gather her baby in her arms.

Ngozi rose with her phone in her hand and walked over to one of the bay windows. She paused at the sight of Alek's mother, LuLu, talking to Alessandra's longtime driver, Roje, in the rear garden. Her eyes widened when he pulled her body close to his by her waist, and she pressed her hands to his broad chest to resist him even as her head tilted back to look up at him.

Ngozi's eyes widened when they shared a passionate kiss that lasted just moments before LuLu broke it and wrenched out of his grasp.

Feeling small for peeking into other people's lives, Ngozi whirled from the window.

Alessandra was breastfeeding Aliyah with a lightweight blanket over her shoulder and the baby to shield herself. "What's wrong?"

"Nothing," Ngozi said, respecting LuLu and Roje's privacy even as her curiosity over the extent of their relationship shifted in overdrive.

As far as she knew, LuLu had never remarried or even dated after the death of her husband, but there was clearly something between her and the handsome middle-aged driver.

Ngozi flipped her phone over.

Ngozi: Welcome back. I can drive. Time?
Chance: 7? I can fix dinner.
Ngozi: Dinner at 7? Dessert by 8? ;-)
Chance: And breakfast in the a.m.?
Ngozi arched a brow at that.
Ngozi: See you at 7, Chance.
Chance: K.

She looked up when the door to the nursery opened and LuLu entered. Only hints of her bright red lipstick remained, with some a little smudged outside the natural lines of her lips. Ngozi bit back a smile. Passion had ruined many lipstick or lip gloss applications for her, as well.

Humph.

Throughout her marriage and for one year after the death of her husband, Ngozi had lived without the passion Chance evoked. And now, just two months into their dalliance, she hungered for him after just a week without it.

"Hello, ladies," LuLu said, setting her tote bag on the floor before heading straight to Alessandra and Aliyah.

"She's all full, LuLu. You can burp her," Alessandra said, rising to hand the baby and a burping cloth over to her mother-in-law.

"How are we doing, ladies?" LuLu asked, lightly patting upward on Aliyah's back as the baby struggled to hold her head up.

Feeling flirty, Ngozi texted Chance.

Ngozi: Panties or no?

Ding-ding.

Chance: Yes…if I can tear them off.

Hmm…

"We were just talking about finding love again after the death of a spouse," Alessandra said, readjusting her maternity bra beneath the rose-gold silk shirt she wore with matching slacks.

Ngozi froze and eyed her client and friend.

Alessandra gave her a deadpan expression.

LuLu looked at Ngozi with a sad smile. "I lost my Kwame six years ago," she began, shifting Aliyah to sit on her lap. "It felt like a piece of me died with him, so I understand how you feel."

Ngozi looked away, unable to accept her sympathy when the truth was unknown to everyone but herself, shielded by her long-practiced ability to hide imperfections and present what was palatable to everyone else. Guilt twisted her stomach as if its grips were real.

"But our stories are different because I am limited by *obligations*…to children, to the dynasty he helped create, to a marriage of more than twenty years, to class, to my age," she admitted.

Her sadness was clear, and it drew Ngozi's eyes back to hers.

"You have a freedom I do not, Ngozi," she said, raising the baby and pressing her cheek against hers. "Do not waste it."

And right then, Ngozi knew that LuLu Ansah loved Roje and wanted nothing more than to be with him, but felt she could not.

Alessandra stooped down beside where LuLu softly sang a Ghanaian song to the baby and lightly touched her knee. "LuLu," she said softly.

The older woman looked down at her.

"Your obligation as a grown woman who has successfully raised her children and mourned her husband is to yourself," Alessandra said, her eyes filled with sincerity and conviction. "You deserve to be loved again, and I *know* there is a man out there who can and will love you just as much if not more, and nothing—not children, business, class or age—should keep that from you."

LuLu's eyes filled with a myriad of emotions, but above all she seemed curious as to just what Alessandra knew of her life.

Ngozi wondered the same.

Ding-ding.

Chance: I really missed you Go-Go.

Her pulse raced. *Go-Go* was short for *Ngozi*. She had no idea why he insisted on giving her a nickname. She'd never had one.

And secretly she liked it. It was something just for them.

Ngozi: I missed you 2.
Chance: Not fun.
Ngozi: Not expected.
Chance: Not a part of the plan.
Ngozi: No. Not at all.

She awaited another text from him. None came. She checked the time. Three more hours until she was with Chance again. It seemed like forever.

You have a freedom I do not, Ngozi. Do not waste it.

Dinner was forgotten.

Food would not sate their hunger for each other.

Chance feasted on her body like it was his own buffet, kissing her skin, licking and lightly biting her taut nipples, massaging the soft flesh of her buttocks as he lifted her hips high off the bed to bury his face first against her thighs and then her plump mound, before spreading her legs wide to expose the beautiful layers of her femininity. Slowly, with more restraint than he had ever shown in his life, he pleased her with his tongue as he enjoyed her unique scent. His moans were guttural as he sucked her fleshy bud between his lips gently, pulling it in and out of his mouth as if to revive her, but it was her shivers and her moans and the tight grips of her hands on his head and shoulders and the way she arched her hips upward, seeking more, that gave him renewed life.

His body in tune with hers, he knew when her release was near and did not relent, wanting to taste her nectar, feel her vibrations and hear her wild cries. With no compassion for wrecked senses, as she was still shivering and crying out, he entered her with one hard thrust that united them, and he did not one stroke until his own body quivered and then stiffened as he joined her in that sweet chasm, crying out like a wounded beast as he clutched her body. He bit down on the pillow beside her head to muffle his high-pitched cries as he forced himself to continue each deep thrust even though he felt near the edge of madness.

Long afterward they lay there, bodies soaked in sweat, pulses racing, hearts pounding and breaths harshly filling the air as they waited for that kinetic energy they'd created to dissipate and free them.

Snores—evidence of their exhaustion—soon filled the air.

Chance awakened the moment he felt the weight of her body shift the bed. She was already reaching for her clothing. "No, Ngozi," he said, his voice deep and thick with sleep.

She paused in pulling on her lingerie to look back at him over her shoulder. "Huh?" she asked, as she clasped her bra from behind.

"Stay the night," he said, sitting up in bed and reaching over to turn on the bedside lamp.

She shook her head, causing her now-unkempt hair to sway back and forth. "No," she said.

The silence in the room became stilted.

"We haven't shared a night together since Italy," he began, finally broaching the subject he'd wanted to for weeks. "You run home to your parents like a little girl with a curfew."

Her brows dipped as she eyed him over the wrap dress she held in her hands. "What…what—what is this?" she asked, motioning her hand from him to her several times. "When did the rules change, because no one told me."

Chance eyed her, knowing she was right.

"I'm not a little girl with a curfew. I am a grown woman with respect for my parents' home," she said.

"Then maybe it's time for a grown woman to have her own home," he said, bending his knees beneath the sheets and setting his arms on top of them.

"Says the grown man who spends his days frolicking," Ngozi said, her tone hard as she jerked on her dress.

Chance stiffened at the judgment. "Frolicking?" he asked, kicking his legs free of the sheets before he climbed from the bed to stand before her.

"Yes, Mr. Italy today and Cabrera tomorrow and… and…and skiing and sailing…and not doing a damn thing else but working on your body and deepening your tan," she said, motioning with her hand toward his sculpted physique.

"Because my work doesn't look like what you think it should, then I'm just a loaf?" Chance asked. "Because I work smarter and not harder, then I ain't shit because I increased my wealth by a million dollars just yesterday. Did *you*?"

"No. Nope. I did not, Mr. Billionaire, but I spent my holidays working to get the bail reduced on a hundred different pro bono clients of nickel-and-dime crimes so they could spend that time with their families, and for those whom I failed, I paid their bail out of my own pocket," she said, her voice impassioned as she looked up at him. "So, you tell me, Mr. Million-Dollars-in-a-Day, what the hell are you doing with your wealth—and your time and your brilliance—besides creating more opportunities to play and have fun?"

"You have no idea what I do because we don't share every aspect of our lives with each other," he spouted, feeling insulted and belittled.

Ngozi raked the tangles from her hair. "Right."

"And when your life is exhausted and time flies because you are so busy working your nine-to-five—excuse me, your six-to-eight—that you haven't lived, then what?" he asked. "You spend the last years of your life with damn regrets. Well, no thank you. I will live and let live."

"You know what, you don't have to justify your life of leisure to me. Just don't judge me for how I choose to color within the lines," she said, dropping down on the edge of the bed to pull on her heels.

Chance turned from her. "All we do is either fuck or fight," he said, wiping his hand over his mouth.

"Then maybe this has run its course," she said.

He looked at her over his broad shoulder. Their eyes locked. "Maybe it has," he agreed.

Ngozi finished gathering her things. "Goodbye, Chance," she said softly, moving to the door.

He followed behind her, saying nothing but feeling so many things. At the front door, he reached out past her to open it for her, even though the chill of December sent goose bumps racing over his nude form. He stood there looking down at her. "It was fun," he began.

"Until it wasn't," she finished.

He bent his head to press a kiss to her forehead and her cheek. "Goodbye, Go-Go," he whispered near her ear.

And with that, she left his home without looking back.

He stood there until she was safely in her car and had driven away from him.

"Five...four...three...two...one! Happy New Year!"

Ngozi took a sip of her champagne from the second floor of her parents' home as all of the partygoers began to either kiss their mate or join in singing "Auld Lang Syne." The charity dinner/silent auction was an annual event for her parents, and Ngozi had attended for many years with Dennis by her side. Now she turned away from the festivities and the emotions it evoked, making her way to her bedroom suite and gratefully closing the door.

She crossed the sitting room to her bedroom, setting the flute on the eight-drawer dresser. The maid staff had already cleaned her room and turned down the bed. She could barely make out the sounds of the party down below as she stepped out of her heels and unzipped the black sequin dress she wore to let it drop to the floor around her feet.

After washing the makeup from her face and wrapping her head with a silk scarf, she sat on the edge of the bed. Soon the quiet was disturbing. Her thoughts were varied. She shifted between grieving the loss of Dennis and feeling guilt over missing Chance.

Needing an escape from her own thoughts and emotions, Ngozi turned off the lights and snuggled beneath the covers. Her line of vision fell on her iPhone sitting on her bedside table. She snaked her arm from under the thick coverlet to tilt it up. No missed calls or texts.

She rubbed the screen with her thumb, fighting a small inner battle over whether to reach out to Chance or not.

The latter won.

There was no happily-ever-after for her and Chance, so why be with someone you were so very different from? It would be fine if their different outlooks on life didn't cause conflict, but Chance wanted to fly out of the country on a whim and would expect her to be able to do the same. And when he drove them somewhere, his lack of respect for the speed limit was another point of contention. Ngozi Johns the attorney most certainly was not a rule breaker testing the boundaries and risking wasting money on speeding tickets.

Their moments together were either filled with passion or skirmishes.

It was tiring.

She returned the phone to its place and released a heavy sigh as she closed her eyes and hoped that her dreams were a distraction from Chance and not filled with memories of him as they had been over the last week since their divide.

"Five...four...three...two...one! Happy New Year!"

Chance pressed a kiss to the mouth of a woman he'd met just that night at the multilevel Drai's Nightclub on the Las Vegas Strip. He couldn't remember her name, and her mouth tasted of cigarettes and liquor that had soured on her tongue. *Serves me right.*

He turned from her just as the fireworks shot off from Caesar's Palace across the street began to echo around them as they lit up the sky. When he felt her tugging at his arm, he gently disengaged her, closed out his tab with the bottle service girl and made his way out of his own section, leaving her and her friends to have at the abundance of liquor he'd already ordered.

Bzzzzzz.

He paused on the dance floor of the club as his

cell phone vibrated against his chest from the inner pocket of his custom black-on-black tuxedo.

Ngozi?

Chance looked down at the screen. "Mama," he mouthed, accepting his disappointment as he answered her call and made his way to the elevator.

"Feliz Año Nuevo, hijo!" Esmerelda exclaimed.

He smiled. "Happy New Year to you, too," he replied, pressing a finger in his ear to help hear beyond the music and noise of the club and the commotion coming through from his mother's boisterous background. She had remained behind in Cabrera after the Christmas holidays.

Chance looked down at his polished shoes. He'd planned to do so as well, but he'd traveled back to the States because he longed for Ngozi. *And then we fought.*

"I'll call you tomorrow," he said, ending the phone call.

He stood there with the colorful strobe lights playing against his face and the bass of the music seeming to reverberate inside his chest, looked around at the gyrating bodies crowding the space and accepted that it would take more than that to make him forget Ngozi.

Two weeks had passed since Ngozi last spoke to Chance. Fourteen days. Three hundred and thirty-six hours. Twenty thousand one hundred and sixty minutes.

She shook her head and rolled her eyes at her desk

in her office as she looked out at the snow falling down on the city.

She'd been so steadfast in her avoidance of the dynamic Dominican that she'd avoided Alessandra and Alek's estate. She was determined to get Chance Castillo out of her system.

And she was failing at it miserably.

Chance increased the speed and incline on one of the three treadmills in his state-of-the-art exercise room. He picked up the pace as he looked out of the glass wall at the snow steadily piling high on the ground and weighing down the branches of the trees in his spacious backyard. He'd spent the last two weeks cooped up in the house, alternating between exercising and working on his app.

Nothing worked to keep Ngozi out of his thoughts.

Or memories of her out of his bed.

With a grunt and mind filled with determination, he picked up the pace, almost at a full sprint now.

It did absolutely nothing toward his outrunning his desires to have Ngozi Johns back in his life.

"Ngozi."

"Chance."

They shared a brief look before moving away from each other after exchanging stilted pleasantries at a charity art exhibit. She hadn't expected him to be there, and from the look on his face when he first spotted her, he had been just as surprised by her appearance. Her heart felt like it was trying to push its way out of her chest.

Wow. He looks sooo good.

Ngozi gripped the stem of the glass of white wine she sipped, fighting the nervous anxiety she felt. She barely focused on the exhibit as she moved about the gallery. Her eyes kept seeking Chance out. And several times, she'd found his gaze on her already.

That thrilled her beyond measure.

Why are we mad at each other again?

That familiar hum of energy and awareness she felt in his presence was still there. Across the room. Across the divide. When their eyes met, it seemed no one else was in the modern gallery.

Not a soul.

She released a breath into her glass as she trailed her fingertips across her collarbone and turned from the sight of him. She soon glanced back. He was gone. She took a few steps in each direction as she searched for him.

What if?

What if they never argued?

What if they were not so intrinsically different? Then what?

Sex, sex and more sex. And fun.

She couldn't deny that Chance had brought plenty of joy into her life. With him, she had laughed more and done a lot more *things*.

Her clit throbbed like it agreed with her naughty thoughts.

Humph.

Ngozi shook her head. "Where did he go?" she mouthed to herself.

She could clearly envision herself walking up to him and requesting that he take her home. And then staying there with him for days on end, whether making love or watching those 1990s action movies they both enjoyed or jogging together or cooking together. Anything. Everything. With him.

Maybe I should go.

Her longing was so strong, and she wasn't quite confident in her willpower.

She took a final sip of her wine and stopped a uniformed waiter to set the goblet on his tray with a smile of thanks. Tucking her gold metallic clutch under her arm, she turned and walked right into a solid chest. "Sorry," she said as a pair of hands gripped her upper arms to steady her.

Warm masculine hands.

She inhaled the scent of cologne.

Both were all too familiar.

Chance.

She knew it before she tilted her head back and looked up into his handsome face.

Chance couldn't remember Ngozi ever looking so beautiful to him. She was stunning in the winter-white jumpsuit she wore with her hair pulled back into a sleek ponytail. The contrast against her skin was amazing.

He hadn't been able to take his eyes off her.

Nor could she him.

Finally, he had to close the distance between them. Now he hesitated to take his hands off her.

And he knew in his gut if he pulled her into a dark secluded corner and pressed his lips to that delicate dip above her collarbone—her spot—that she would not resist him. Once again, she would be his. But for how long? A few stolen moments? One night?

"We can't avoid each other," Chance said, finally dropping his hands from her arms as his heart beat wildly.

"We spoke," she said, taking a step back from him as she smoothed her hand over her head and dragged it down her waist-length ponytail.

Chance nodded. "We did."

They fell silent.

"I thought this wasn't your type of thing?" Ngozi said.

"Art?" Chance asked.

"No, charity," she said with a sly lift of her brows and a "so there" look.

Chance frowned. "Still throwing jabs, huh?"

"Yes, that was childish, Chance. My bad," she admitted.

"As a matter of fact, I am sponsoring this event," Chance said, trying his best not to sound smug or give her the same "so there" look.

She looked perplexed. "Did the Ansahs know about that?"

He nodded. "Yes. I wish they could be here. Alek helped me arrange the connection."

"Well, they claimed they couldn't make it so I was

pressed to use their ticket…with no mention of your involvement, of course."

Chance rocked on his heels and looked up at the well-lit ceiling as he chuckled. "Scheming, huh?" he asked, looking back at her.

Their eyes locked before she looked away with a bite of her bottom lip that stirred naughty thoughts in him.

"It seems so," Ngozi said, her nervousness clear.

"You were right," he said.

"About?"

"Me needing to do more. Care more. Focus more on what's right," he admitted, his eyes searching her face for a sign that she understood this shift in his thinking was due to her.

She looked surprised. "You did this for me?" she asked.

He shook his head. "No, I didn't know you were coming, remember, *but* I took your advice, Ngozi, and it feels good to give back more, Mrs. Pro Bono."

Her shoulders slumped a bit as she looked up at him in wonder.

Chance balled his hands into fists behind his back to beat off the temptation to stroke her face. "What's that look about, Ngozi?" he asked.

Tears filled her eyes, and his gut felt wrenched. She tried valiantly to blink them away before turning to quickly stride away.

He fell in step with her and placed an arm around her shoulder to guide her into an office. "Ngozi," he said softly, wanting her to open up to him.

She shook her head. "I feel silly, but... I appreciate your taking my advice and listening to me even though I voiced it out of anger. Outside of my career, what I care about, what I think...what I *feel*," she stressed, letting the rest of her words fade as she pinched the bridge of her nose and closed her eyes.

Chance could no longer resist, stepping close to pull her into his embrace. When she allowed him to do so and rested her forehead against his chest as she released a long breath before her body relaxed, he enjoyed being someone she could rely on for comfort and support.

"You just don't know, Chance," she admitted softly.

He set his chin on her head lightly. "Tell me. You can talk to me about anything, Ngozi. I promise you that," he swore, surprised by the truth of his own words.

He wanted so badly, in that moment, to inquire if her husband had been that for her. Her protector. Her warrior. Her shoulder to lean on.

But he did not.

"Chance Castillo, I don't know what to do with you," she professed.

The same struggle he felt between what he wanted and what he needed was there in her voice. "Help me become a better man."

She looked up at him. "And what will you do with me?" she asked, her hands snaking around his waist to settle on his back.

"Help you color out of the lines a little bit more."

She smiled. "And somewhere in the middle—"

"We have amazing sex."

"Chance," she chided softly.

"Ngozi," he volleyed back.

She chuckled.

He looked down at her, studied her, enjoyed the beauty of her. *She is not Helena.*

The truth was Ngozi Johns was not the type of woman built for frivolity. She was "it"—fun, brilliant, sexy, loyal, reliable, empathetic…

He could go on and on.

But what if I'm wrong?

"Let's stop fighting this, Ngozi," he implored, touching his index finger to the base of her chin to lift her head high as he bent his legs to lower himself and touch his lips down upon hers.

Her answer, he was pleased to note, was to tightly grip his shirt in her hands as she kissed him back with the passion he had craved and missed.

Chapter 7

Ngozi was exhausted.

From the moment they left the art gallery together, she and Chance hadn't been able to keep their hands—or anything else—off each other.

In the office at the gallery.

In the car.

Against the wall of the living room.

On the bench of his nine-foot Steinway grand piano in the music room.

In the shower.

And the bed...where he held her nude body closely as he united them with deep intense strokes and whispered to her how much he missed her until they climaxed and cried out in sweet release together.

And she was spent as she straddled Chance's

strong thighs as he sat in the middle of his bed with his back pressed against the headboard. Her sigh was inevitable when he gripped her thighs to massage them. She rested her hands on his shoulders, gently kneading the muscles there.

"We're really doing this?" Ngozi asked, pressing kisses to his brow as he lowered his head to her chest.

"I don't think we can resist," Chance said, turning his face from one side to the other to plant a warm kiss to each curve of her breasts.

She eased her hands from his shoulders and up his neck to grip his face to tilt upward until he was looking at her. The room was dimly lit by a corner lamp across the room, but the light of the moon and the brightness of the white snow reflected a light in his eyes that she felt herself getting lost in. He met her stare and she lost her breath, feeling something tugging at her heart and claiming a piece of her soul.

She kissed him lightly. "Chance," she whispered, her eyes searching his as she felt a lightness in her chest.

Bzzzzzz.

They both looked to his iPhone vibrating on his bedside table.

Ngozi was thankful for the intrusion. She had started to feel spellbound.

Chance held one of her butt cheeks with one hand and reached for his phone with the other.

She felt his body stiffen. "What's wrong?"

"The attorney notified me that Helena has been officially served her summons," Chance said, his voice hard as he turned the phone to show her.

Ngozi winced. *Helena.*

She moved to rise up off him, but he wrapped his arm around her waist and held her closer. "Don't answer that, Chance," she advised, putting on her attorney hat.

She visualized the blonde Cuban with whom he'd been ready to share his life. Ngozi, educated woman and accomplished attorney, had looked up the woman's Instagram account weeks ago. She was gorgeous. J-Lo level.

"Helena," he said, his tone chilly enough to make her wish for a sweater.

"You have got to be kidding me, Chance. Are you serious? Suing me?" she railed.

He had her on speaker.

Ngozi successfully freed herself from his hold and rose from the bed, not interested in eavesdropping on their conversation.

"Racking up a million dollars' worth of bills for a wedding while screwing another man? Are *you* serious?" he countered, his anger and annoyance clear.

Ngozi paused in the entrance to his bathroom and looked back at him over his shoulder. Something in him needed this moment with Helena.

She squinted as he began to slash his hands across the air as he rose from the bed and paced, and they began arguing heatedly in Spanish.

Her entire body went warm and she leaned against

the frame of the doorway as she accepted what she was feeling. Jealousy. Pure and simple.

And she knew that when she looked in his eyes and saw the moonlight in the brown depths, that the emotion that took her breath was the same one that made her warm with envy.

Her heart pounded so loudly it felt like it thudded in her ears.

Ngozi gripped the door frame tightly and released a long, shaky breath as the truth of her feelings settled in…and scared her.

I love him. I love Chance.

"Go to hell!" Helena screamed.

Ngozi refocused her attention on them.

"I will see you there," Chance returned coldly, holding the phone close to his mouth.

Ngozi stiffened her back and pushed off the door frame to walk across his expansive bedroom and calmly slip the phone out of his hand to end the call. She turned and tossed it onto the middle of his bed. "It is hurtful to your case to argue with Ms. Guzman," she said, turning away from him so he couldn't see how hurtful it was to her, as well.

How did I let this happen?

"You're right," he said.

She glanced at him as she gathered her clothing, taking note with a critical eye that he stood before the floor-to-ceiling windows with his hands on his hips as he looked out at his backyard. His back was to her, but in his reflection in the glass, she took in both his nudity and the pensive look on his face.

He looked lost in thought.

She was tempted to dress and walk out, leaving him lost.

Instead, she set her clothes down on the edge of the bed and walked over to him to press her body against his back and wrap her arms around him as she pressed a kiss to his spine.

Chance brought one hand up to cover hers as he looked down at her over his shoulder. "I'm glad you're back," he said.

Ngozi eased her body around his to stand before him with her bare bottom, her upper back and head against the chilly glass as she looked up at him. "You sure?" she asked, reaching up to stroke his low-cut beard.

Chance cupped her face with his hands, tilting her face up as he bent his head to kiss her. "Honestly?" he asked, as his eyes searched hers just as hers had searched his earlier.

She wondered if he felt the same breathlessness that she had in that moment. "Always," she finally answered, her voice whisper soft.

"I wasn't looking for anything serious and…and I'm not sure I'm ready," Chance admitted. "In fact, I don't think either of us are."

She nodded with a slight smile. "True," she confessed, enjoying the feel of his hands.

Chance stroked her lip with his thumb. "But I don't know how to be without you, Ngozi. I've tried and failed. Twice."

More truth.

The hour was late. Later than she'd ever stayed at Chance's home, but when their simple kisses filled with heat and passion, she didn't dare to resist. Once she stroked him to hardness, in tune to her soft sucking motions of his tongue, the chill of the glass against her body faded as the heat of their passion reigned. She wrapped her arms around his neck and her legs around his waist after he hoisted her body up, centered her core above his upright hardened length and lowered her body down on each inch until they were united fully.

Ngozi gasped and released a tiny cry as she arched her back, pushing her small but plump breasts forward. Chance licked at each of her taut brown nipples with a low growl as she rotated her hips in an up-and-down motion like a rider on a mechanical bull. She kept looking at him, enjoying the glaze of pleasure in his eyes, the grimace of intensity and the quick shallow breaths through pursed lips as he fought for control.

"Ahhhh," she sighed, her eyes still locked on him as she released his neck to press the back of her hands against the glass and slid them upward as she continued to wind her hips.

Chance's grip on her hips deepened, and she felt him harden even more inside her.

"Yes," she sighed with a grunt of pleasure, closing her eyes as she tilted her head back.

Never had she felt so bold, so sexy, so powerful as she did with Chance. The look in his eyes, the strength of his hold and his reaction to her moves pushed her beyond her normal limits with her sexuality. It was new and refreshing and satisfying in every way.

With him there was no shame. No inhibitions. No denial of her wants and desires.

With him she was free.

With the strength of her thigh muscles from her daily runs, Ngozi gripped his waist tighter and lowered her body down the glass until they were face-to-face. They locked eyes and shared what seemed to be a dozen small kisses as he took the lead, alternating between a deep thrust and a circular rotation of his hips that caused his stiff inches to touch every bit of her feminine core and drag against her throbbing bud.

And there against the chilly glass, with the heat they created steaming away the frost, Chance stroked them to another explosive climax that shook Ngozi to her core with such beauty and pleasure that it evoked tears.

She felt like she was free-falling.

It was amazing.

Still shivering, she clung to Chance and buried her face against his neck as he walked them over to his bed. She relaxed into the softness of the bed and snuggled one of the down pillows under her head. She closed her eyes as the exhaustion of her emotions and her climax defeated her.

"You're staying?" Chance asked, his surprise swelling in his voice.

She nodded as he curved his body to hers and

wrapped a strong arm around her waist after pulling a cool cotton sheet over them.

Ngozi snuggled down deeper on the bed, content that she didn't have the will or the energy to leave him.

It was early morning before Ngozi made the short trip home from Alpine to Passion Grove. She entered her security code on the side entrance in the massive kitchen, pushing it open as a yawn escaped her mouth. Chance had gifted her another mind-blowing, energy-sapping, eyes-crossing orgasm before she left him.

"No sleep last night?"

Startled, she paused in the doorway at her father sitting at the mahogany island, still in his plaid robe and pajamas, drinking from a cup of what she presumed to be coffee from the heavy scent of it in the air. "Sir?" she asked, by way of stalling as her nerves were instantly rattled.

"We're not trying to heat the outdoors, Ngozi."

Her head whipped to the right to find her mother at the breakfast nook, also in her nightclothes as she drummed her clear-coated fingernails atop the round table.

Double trouble.

Ngozi turned to close the door, pausing to lick her lips as she furrowed her brows. She felt like a child about to be scolded.

"Reeds was kind enough to let us know you called and told him you were staying in the city for the night at the firm's apartment," her father began, ever the attorney—retired or not.

Late last night, she had dug her phone out of the pile of clothing on the floor and texted Reeds to cover for her yet again. "Good, I wouldn't want you to worry," she said, striding across the kitchen at a pace that could have won a speed-walking race with ease.

"Ngozi," her mother said, all simple and easy.

Deceptive as hell.

Ngozi paused and turned, uncomfortable with her face makeup-free and her hair disheveled, dressed in the same white outfit she'd worn to the art gallery the night before.

"Your father is retired from the firm but he's still the majority owner, my daughter," Val said, turning on the padded bench to fold her legs and look across the distance at her daughter. "And that includes the firm's apartment—"

Oh damn.

She was a gifted attorney as well and knew exactly where she had made a wrong calculation. Her eyes shifted from one to the other. Her father took another drink, and in that moment, Ngozi wished he would stir his spoon in his cup so the floor would open and send her to her own special sunken place.

They know I wasn't there.

"Who is he?" Horace asked, setting the cup down on top of the island.

Ngozi opened her mouth to lie. When it came to her relationship with her parents, subterfuge was her first line of defense.

Val held up a hand. "Let's remember that anything less than the truth is disrespect," she advised before shifting her focus back to her husband.

"Who is he?" Horace repeated.

I don't want to lie. I don't want to deny Chance. I don't want to.

"Chance Castillo," she said, physically and mentally steeling herself for a long list of questions and reminders of obligations to Dennis even beyond his death.

Silence reigned.

Their faces were unreadable.

"Invite him to dinner," her mother said.

Ngozi grimaced. "But—"

"Soon," her father added before returning his attention to his coffee.

"Horace, we better go up and get ready," Val said, rising from her seat. "We have that breakfast meeting with possible donors for my upcoming campaign."

Ngozi looked from one to the other, her mouth slightly ajar. She couldn't hide her shock, even as they eased past her to leave her in the kitchen alone.

Chance carefully steered his silver Bentley Bentayga SUV over the busy New Jersey streets, being sure to stay focused with all of the snow and ice on the ground. As he pulled the vehicle to a stop at a red traffic light, he looked over at Ngozi sitting beside him in the passenger seat. He smiled at all the nervous gestures he spotted. Swaying her knee back and forth.

Twisting the large diamond-encrusted dome ring she wore on her index finger. Nibbling on her bottom lip.

He had picked her up from work, fresh off yet another trial win, and she was dressed in a claret ostrich feather coat with a turtleneck and pencil leather skirt of the same shade that was beautiful against her mocha complexion, particularly with the deep mahogany lipstick she wore.

"Mi madre no muerde, sabes," he said, giving her thigh a warm rub and squeeze as he steered forward under the green traffic light with his other hand.

"She doesn't bite, huh?" Ngozi said, translating his words. Inside the dimly lit interior of the SUV, she glanced at him with a weak smile. "I told you my parents want to meet you as well, so let's see how easy-breezy you are when I finally get the nerve to serve you up to them."

"I'm ready," Chance said with a chuckle as he turned onto the short paved drive of his mother's two-story brick home just a few miles from his estate. He pressed the button to open the door of the two-car garage and pulled into the empty spot next to her red convertible Mercedes Benz she called "Spicy."

"And the deposition tomorrow—are you ready for that?" Ngozi asked.

Chance shut the SUV off and looked over at her. The overhead motion lighting of the garage lit up the car, offering him a clearer view of her face. "Yes, I am."

"That's good," she said. "Just be sure to keep your cool."

He frowned. They rarely discussed his lawsuit against Helena. "My cool?"

Ngozi reached for the handle to the passenger door. She looked nonplussed. "Same advice I would give if you were still my client," she said matter-of-factly with a one-shoulder shrug.

"But you're not my attorney, you're my woman," he reminded her.

Ngozi relaxed back against the seat. She stroked the underside of his chin, letting the short beard hairs prick against her hand. "Your woman, huh?" she asked.

He smiled as he leaned in and pressed his lips to her own as he reached down to use the controls to lower her seat backward.

"Don't…start…something…we…can't…finish," she whispered up to him in between kisses as her eyes studied his.

"Who says we can't—"

"Chance! Are you coming in?"

They froze before they sat straight up in their separate chairs again.

Chance looked through the windshield at his mother standing in the open doorway leading from the garage into her kitchen. She was squinting as she peered into the car with a frown.

Ngozi covered her face with her hands, feeling the warmth of embarrassment that rose in her cheeks. "Oh God," she moaned.

Chance chuckled before he opened the driver's side door. "We're headed right in," he called out to her.

She turned and walked back into the house, leaving the door ajar.

"Great first impression," Ngozi drawled, before he climbed from the car and strode around the front to open the passenger door.

"No worries, *mi tentadora*," he said, closing the door when she stepped aside.

"Your temptress?" she asked, looking back at him as she climbed the brick staircase.

Yes, you are.

A relationship had not been in the cards for him after Helena, but Ngozi had drawn him in from their first meeting and he hadn't been able to shake his desire for her ever since. She was his temptation. His temptress.

And in time, his acceptance of that truth shook him to his core.

"Ready?" he asked, seeing the nervousness in her eyes as she waited for him to pull the glass door open for her.

She nodded before stepping inside.

Chance eyed his mother as she turned and walked across the spacious kitchen with a wide, warm smile.

"Welcome, welcome," Esmerelda said, grasping Ngozi's shoulders as she kissed both of her cheeks. "It's nice to meet you."

Chance eyed Ngozi as she returned the warmth, and her shoulders relaxed.

Their exchange pleased him.

"We can go in to eat since you were running a little behind," she said, with a meaningful stare at Chance.

He gave her a wide smile. Her disapproval vanished.

"What do you want me to carry, Ma?" Chance asked.

"Nothing, just go on in."

Chance led Ngozi out of the kitchen and through to the dining room. The large wood table, covered with a beautiful lace tablecloth that looked out of place among the modern design of the home, was set for three with his mother's favorite crystal drink ware and a large floral arrangement. "She went all out," he said as he pulled back the chair for Ngozi at the table.

She took the seat, smiling up at him when he stroked her neck before moving around the table to take the chair across from her.

"Relax," he mouthed as his mother began carrying in large ceramic bowls in bright colors to set on the table.

The smell of the food intensified, and Chance's stomach rumbled.

"I'm too nervous to eat," she admitted.

"Nervous? Why?" Esmerelda asked, setting down a bowl of white rice and a pitcher of amber-colored liquid with fresh fruit pieces.

"Nothing, Ms. Castillo," Ngozi said.

Chance fought not to wince as his mother gave her a stiff smile. "It's Ms. Diaz," she said with emphasis. "Castillo is the name of his father, who didn't choose to share it with me by marriage."

Ngozi remained silent, giving Chance a pointed

stare as his mother took her seat at the head of the table.

"She didn't know, Ma," he said, reaching to remove the lid from the bright turquoise tureen. "*Tayota guisada con longaniza.* I love it."

"This is a popular dish from my country," Esmerelda said, scooping a heaped spoonful of rice into each of three bowls stacked by her place setting. She handed each bowl to Chance to ladle the sausage and chayote cooked in tomato sauce, onion, garlic, cilantro and bell peppers. "I hope you don't find it *too* spicy. Sometimes the palate of those not raised in our culture is delicate."

Chance frowned. Traditionally, there wasn't much heat to the dish.

"I'm sure it's fine. Everything looks delicious," Ngozi said, using both of her hands to accept the bowl he handed her.

He picked up his spoon and dug in, enjoying the flavor of the food. There was a little bit of a spicy kick that tickled even his tongue.

Ngozi coughed.

He glanced across the table at her. Sweat beads were on her upper lip and forehead. Her eyes were glassy from tears.

She coughed some more.

Chance rushed to fill her glass with his mother's homemade fruit juice, standing to reach across the table and press it into her hands.

Ngozi drank from it in large gulps.

"I'm so sorry, Ngozi. Perhaps I can fix you something else if that is too much for you," Esmerelda said, sounding contrite.

Ngozi cleared her throat. "No, this is delicious," she said, setting the glass down before dabbing her upper lip with the cloth napkin she'd opened across her lap.

Chance shook his head. "You don't have to—"

"This is fine," she said, giving him a hard stare and his mother a soft smile before taking a smaller bite of the dish from her bowl.

As their meal continued in silence, Chance eyed Ngozi taking small bites of food followed by large sips of juice. It was clear she didn't want to offend his mother.

"Ngozi, Chance tells me you're an attorney," Esmerelda said, covering her nearly empty bowl with her cloth napkin as she placed her elbows on the table and looked directly at Ngozi.

"Yes, I'm a junior partner of the firm my father established," she answered.

"My Chance seems to have a soft spot for attorneys," she said.

Ngozi licked her lips as she set her napkin on the table.

"Helena and Ngozi are nothing alike," Chance offered into the stilted silence.

"Espero que no, por tu bien," Esmerelda said. *"Ella debería estar llorando a su esposo y no buscando uno nuevo. Los buscadores de oro huelen el dinero como tiburones huelen a sangre."*

"Ma," he snapped sharply as he sat up straight in the chair and eyed her in surprise and disappointment.

He could hardly believe her words and could only imagine how harsh they sounded to Ngozi: *"I hope not for your sake. She should be grieving her husband and not looking for a new one. Gold diggers smell money like sharks smell blood."* Ngozi rose to her feet, looking down at his mother. Chance rose, as well.

"Se equivoca acerca de mí, Señora Díaz," Ngozi said.

His mother's jaw tightened, and her eyes widened in surprise to find Ngozi speak in fluent Spanish to proclaim that she was wrong about her.

Chance shook his head. He agreed with Ngozi that his mother was mistaken about her.

"I am not a gold digger nor am I on the prowl to replace my dead husband with a new one," she said in his mother's native tongue, her voice hollow.

Chance eyed his mother in disbelief. He could tell she felt his stare as she avoided his look.

"My apologies if I offended you," Esmerelda said, reverting to English.

"Thank you for dinner," Ngozi said before quickly turning to walk into the kitchen. Soon the alarm system announced the opening and closing of the side entrance door.

Chance's eyes continued to bore into her.

"What?" she asked.

"You have never taught me or shown me the example of how to be rude and mean to anyone," he began. "I'm just trying to figure out who is sitting before me."

Esmerelda turned in her chair and looked up at him. "I watched you recover from heartbreak by Ese Rubio Diablo for almost a year, so what you see now is a mother willing to fight to make sure you don't go through that heartache again," she said, her voice impassioned and her eyes lit with the fire of determination.

"I know you mean well, but Ngozi should not have to suffer for what Helena did to me," Chance insisted, forcing softness into his tone. "All I ask is that you give her the same kindness you give strangers. Even a dog deserves respect, Ma."

She shrugged and turned her lips downward.

He stepped near her and bent at the waist to press a kiss to the top of her head. "Thank you for dinner," he said and then frowned deeply as he rose to look down at her again in skepticism. "Did you spice the food on purpose?"

Esmerelda sucked air between her teeth and threw her hands up. "It didn't kill her," she said.

"Ma!"

"What?"

"I'll see you later," Chance said, walking around her chair. He paused. "Do you need anything?"

"Just for you to be happy," Esmerelda said.

"I'm a grown man. My happiness is in my hands now," he said. "You don't have to work double shifts to take care of me and send me to private school. I will love you and spoil you because of your sacrifice, but your time putting me before yourself is over. I got it from here."

She remained quiet and studied her nails.

He could tell she was hurt, but the truth of his words could not be retracted to save her feelings. He gave his mother the world, but he was a man who had no desire to be babied and coddled by his mother.

"Te amo, Ma."

"I love you, too, Chance."

With that he took his leave.

Ngozi was sitting in the SUV. He eyed her through the windshield as he made his way over to the driver's side door. He climbed inside. Unspoken words swelled between them.

Chance licked his lips and reached over to take one of her soft hands in his. "Say it," he urged. "I'm listening."

"It's nothing. I'm fine," she said, looking to him with a smile as fake as the plastic one pinned onto a Mr. Potato Head toy.

"Don't ever deny your feelings for the sake of anyone—not me or anyone else—because they matter," he said.

She smiled again. It was soft and genuine. "I wouldn't know what it feels like to put myself first," she admitted.

Chance leaned over to press kisses to the side of her face. "Try it," he whispered into her ear.

"I want you to know that I am not looking to replace Dennis," she said, turning on the seat to face him. "Hell, I don't even feel I have the right to move on and be happy when he's dead."

Chance took a moment to properly frame what he said next. "I never expect you to let go of Dennis."

She began to stroke his hand. "Not of him, of my guilt," she acknowledged before closing her eyes and releasing a breath.

He wondered if talking about him was like releasing steam to dissolve the buildup of pressure.

"We've never spoken of his death," he offered, being sure to tread lightly to avoid stepping on or disrespecting her feelings.

"I've never talked about it with anyone."

Her sadness was palpable, and his gut ached for her. "And do you want to talk now?" he asked.

Ngozi shook her head. "Not yet, but thank you for letting me know that someone is there to finally listen to me."

"Sounds like a lot to unload from that clever brain of yours," he said, his eyes searching his.

"It is. Think you can handle it?"

With a final kiss, he turned his attention to starting the car. "For you I will do anything," he said, letting the truth of his words settle in his chest as the engine roared to life.

Chapter 8

No, Ngozi. No.

Determined not to give in to her own curiosity, she pushed back from her desk and crossed her arms over her chest. Her eyes stayed locked on her computer monitor, though. She had to tighten her fingers into a fist, hoping to stop herself from reaching out and pulling up the video recording of the deposition of Helena Guzman in Chance's lawsuit against her.

No.

Ngozi had been in court all morning and missed when Helena and her attorney arrived. She considered it a mixed blessing.

Grabbing the edge of her desk, she rolled the few inches forward and picked up her pen. Even as she reviewed the case file in front of her, her attention kept shifting to her monitor. *To hell with it.*

Ngozi reached for the keyboard.

"Ms. J."

She jumped like a startled deer, rising and then dropping back down in her seat. Angel looked at her in bewilderment. She cleared her throat and pressed her palms down on the desk. "Yes, Angel?" she asked, thankful for the black shirt and simple wide-leg slacks the young lady wore.

She'd really been making an effort of late to tame her wild ways and boisterous unprofessional behavior. Ngozi took note, appreciated it and was proud of her.

Angel walked in the room, looking nervous as she set an envelope before her.

"What's this?" Ngozi said, opening the flap to find a check.

"I finally saved enough to repay you for my fine and the bond that you paid," Angel said with a wide smile. "And that's the first check I ever wrote from my new checking account, ya heard me."

Ngozi was stunned and she sat back in her chair, letting the check and the envelope drop to the desk as she pressed her fingertips to her lips. There was no denying the pride on Angela's face. And it was the reason she fought just as hard for her pro bono cases as all her others. The hope of giving someone a second chance to better their lives. To find a better way. And in truth, out of all the clients she went above and beyond her attorney duties for, she wouldn't have guessed that Angel would be such a success story.

"If it wasn't for you, I would still be stripping and tricking. Now I'm looking up to you, and I ain't gonna never be no lawyer or nothing, but I want to go back to school…because of you. So thank you for seeing something in me 'cause it taught me to see more in myself, Ms. J.," Angel said.

Ngozi felt emotional, but she kept her face neutral. Maintained her professionalism.

Stuck to her routine—her facade.

Don't ever deny your feelings for the sake of anyone—not me or anyone else—because they matter.

Taking a breath, she rose from her seat and came around the desk to pull Angel into a tight hug. "I'm so proud of you," she said, letting her emotions swell in her tone. "Keep it up."

"I will, Ms. J. I won't let you down," she promised.

Ngozi nodded, releasing her as she stepped back. "I believe that. Thank you," she said, turning to reclaim her seat behind her desk.

Angel took her leave with one last little wave.

"Shut the door, please," she requested, already turning her attention back to her wireless keyboard.

Ngozi was left with her curiosity about the deposition still nagging at her. With a bite of her bottom lip, she logged on to the company's server and searched for the video file of the deposition. She stroked her chin and released long steady breaths at the sight of Chance and his attorney, Larry Rawlings, entering one of the three conference rooms in the offices of Vincent and Associates Law.

Her heart raced at the sight of Chance. The night before, they had lain naked together in front of his lit fireplace as she worked on a new case and he read a book. Leaving him to return to Passion Grove had not been easy, especially because she knew his deposition was the next day.

Now here she sat looking on like a Peeping Thomasina at his ex, a blonde and beautiful golden-skinned Afro-Cuban, entering the room with her attorney. She was rattled. She and Helena were completely different in looks, and although Ngozi was a confident woman, it would be hard to deny Helena's stunning beauty…or the way Chance stared at her with such livid intensity.

Ngozi's heart was pounding as she looked on.

"Ms. Guzman, were you actively involved in a relationship with Jason Young while planning your wedding to my client, Chance Castillo?" Larry asked, looking across the table at the woman over the rim of his horn-rimmed glasses.

Larry's slightly disheveled appearance and his brilliance didn't align, which caught most people unfamiliar with him off guard.

Helena conferred with her attorney before giving Larry a cool look. "No. It was not a relationship," she said, her accent present.

Chance loudly scoffed.

Helena continued to ignore him.

Ngozi nibbled on her bottom lip.

Larry made a note on his notepad. "Were you and Mr. Young intimate during that time? Did you share meals? Did you vacation together? Did you have conversations about life? Did you ever discuss your future with him?"

Helena again conferred with her attorney, a tall silver-haired woman with an olive complexion. "Per the advice of my counsel, I am invoking my right under the Fifth Amendment not to answer, on the grounds I may incriminate myself."

Ngozi winced when Chance jumped up out of his seat. "If I were you, I wouldn't admit to being a scheming two-timing—"

Larry rose to his feet and whispered in Chance's ear.

Both men took their seats.

Ngozi barely heard the rest of their words because of her focus on how Helena barely glanced in Chance's direction, but he never took his eyes off her. His hostility toward Helena seemed to swell and fill the room. Long after the deposition ended and the video faded to black, Ngozi couldn't forget the look in his eyes or the tense stance of his frame.

Sadness and jealousy stung with the sharpness of a needle. His demeanor gave credence to Helena's response that the motivation for Chance's lawsuit was irrational hurt brought on by a broken heart, and even more, injured pride.

His anger was immense, and she felt his hurt was equal to it. As was the love he'd once had for her.

Love he doesn't have for me.

His anger leaves no room in his heart for anything else.

For a long time, she sat staring out the window with that thought foremost in her mind.

The dry heat of the sauna radiated against their nude frames as Ngozi sat astride Chance's lap on one of the cedar benches lining the large infrared sauna. The red light cast their bronzed bodies with a glow meant to be therapeutic, but which also gave the warm interior a vibe that was sexy.

"Talk to me, Ngozi."

Chance was stroking her back. He felt her stiffen for a millisecond before her body relaxed against his again. They'd decided to enjoy a sauna while a three-star Michelin chef who now worked exclusively as a private chef prepared them a romantic dinner. It was clear to him that her mind was elsewhere from the moment she had arrived at his estate.

As much as he enjoyed the feel of her soft body pressed against the hard muscles of his frame, it was clear that a conversation was more needed than another session of fiery sex in a steamy room beneath a red light.

She took a large breath that caused her chest to rise and fall as she sat up straight to look down into his face with serious eyes. "I don't think I have a right to ask, because I know that I'm not where I should be with the death of my husband…and who am I to expect something from you that I can't seem to claim for myself?"

Chance felt lost in her gaze. "And what is that?" he asked, massaging her buttocks.

"Moving beyond. Letting go," she admitted with several soft nods as if to reaffirm her words to herself.

He remembered the moment they shared in his SUV the night he brought her to dinner at his mother's. "About your guilt?"

She looked unsure. "Yes…my guilt about Dennis… and whether you could drop your lawsuit against Helena?" she asked, forcing her words out in a rush because of the courage it took for her to finally voice her worries.

Chance frowned, and his hands paused on her bottom. "You want me to drop the lawsuit?" he asked, his surprise clear.

Ngozi looked away from him as she nodded.

He gently touched her chin and guided her face forward so that their eyes were locked once more. "What's going on? Do you think I'll lose? Is this about us? What…what's going on?" he asked, his tone soft.

Ngozi gave him a soft smile, looking up at the red light before glancing back at him. "Did you mean it when you said I could tell you anything?"

"Absolutely, Ngozi. Anything," he emphasized, as a dozen or more questions about the legal validity of his case raced through his head.

"I have never told anyone that my marriage was not at all what it appeared to be," she began, withdrawing her hands from his body as she bent her arms and pressed her hands to the back of her neck. "I think we were meant to be friends rather than spouses, because in the end this person with whom I had once enjoyed spending time began to feel like an…an…adversary."

Ngozi tilted her head, exposing the smooth expanse of her neck as she closed her eyes and released a long breath.

He remained quiet, wanting her to unload her feelings.

"In law school we worked together to study, pass tests and graduate, but soon our careers seemed to take us in two different directions, and all of a sudden, we were cold and distant with each other, and the only heat was in arguments, but then we would put on the greatest show alive like circus monkeys and pretend in public. All smiles. All kisses. All lovey-dovey bull. Nothing but icing covering up shit."

She looked off into the distance, but the pain in her eyes was clear. "We were in our apartment one Sunday and we were both preparing for cases the next day. He was in our office, and I was in the living room on the floor in front of the fireplace. I was feeling weary and decided to make coffee. I made him a cup just the way he liked, black and sweet, in this huge Superman mug that he'd had since like high school," she said softly, as if back in the moment. "I took the coffee in to him and he didn't look up at me or say thank you. I don't know, in that moment I was so sick of the silence and the distance and the way we were with each other. I missed my friend and I *felt* like I hated my husband—and they were one in the same man."

Chance noticed she was raking the tips of her fingernails against her neck, and he reached up to take her hand into his. She seemed so lost in her thoughts that he wondered if she even noticed.

"In that moment I just wanted him out of the apartment, out of my sight. Just gone," she said, her expression becoming pained. "I asked him to go get lunch, just to get him out…and…and he *never* came back."

Her body tensed, and she winced as a tear raced down her cheek, quickly followed by another and another.

Chance's heart ached for her. "What happened, Ngozi?" he asked, his voice tempered.

"A car crash," she said. "I wished he was gone. I wanted our marriage over. I sent him out. And he never came back. And I have never told a soul," she admitted in a harsh whisper.

"Oh, baby, you can't put the weight of his death on your conscience or your shoulders like that," Chance said, pressing his hands to her face.

She nodded. "My brain understands that, but I still feel like I don't deserve to be so happy."

"With me?" he asked.

Ngozi looked at him. "You were the last thing I was looking for, Chance Castillo," she admitted. "And now I wonder just what I would do without you."

His heart swelled and filled with an emotion for her that had become familiar of late. An emotion he was still hesitant to claim but was finding hard to deny.

I love her.

His heart pounded furiously.

"Do you still love Helena?"

His brows dipped. "No," he said unequivocally.

I love you.

"Then why the lawsuit, Chance?" Ngozi asked. "It keeps you connected to her. It keeps you angry at her."

He stiffened, feeling uneasy. "I'm not—"

"I saw the video of the deposition, Chance."

He swallowed the rest of his denial, closing his eyes to avoid her gaze on him. Yes, Helena had infuriated him earlier in the deposition. That was undeniable. "It was my first time seeing her since she walked out on me before the wedding," he admitted, giving her the same glimpse into his vulnerability that she'd given him. "All I could think about when I was looking at her is how much she'd fooled me. Made a fool of me. It took me back to being the poor kid at school with the rich kids, with girls who looked a lot like Helena, who wouldn't give me the time of day."

Damn.

The thought that childhood issues still affected him stung like crazy.

Ngozi stroked his face and he turned his head toward her touch, enjoying the warmth, care and concern he felt there.

"I'm not dropping the case, Ngozi," he insisted, waiting for her touch to cease.

It didn't.

But she released a heavy breath. "Chance?"

"I don't want her back. I am glad that she didn't marry me and have me financing her side relationship, but it was wasteful and vindictive to push for a huge wedding on my dime when she knew she wasn't all-in, Ngozi. She doesn't just get to walk away with no consequences. She left me holding the bag regarding that wedding."

Ngozi said no more as she rested her forehead against his.

He knew she still held her doubts about his feelings for Helena, and he wanted nothing more than to admit that she had captured the heart he swore he would never entrust to another woman again. But the moment didn't call for it. It would seem more of a ploy than a revelation of his true feelings, so he held back, admitting that he needed time to adjust to the truth himself.

I love Ngozi.

The sound of utensils hitting against flatware echoed into the quiet of the stately dining room as Chance, Ngozi and her parents enjoyed their dinner of prime rib, potatoes au gratin and sautéed string beans.

It was *so* awkward.

Ngozi took a sip of plum wine—a deep one.

"So, Chance, tell me more about your work?" Horace asked, settling back in his chair as he eyed the man sitting to his right.

Ngozi went tense. *Work? Chance spent his downtime planning what to do during his free time.*

"Once I sold my app, I shifted away from finance full-time, and now I have a few different irons in the fire," he said, sounding confident and proud. "I'm a consultant and minority owner of the firm that purchased the app I developed. I do freelance investing for several clients that insisted I continue to work on their portfolios. And I'm currently finishing up a new app to help productivity for businesspeople on the go."

Ngozi sputtered the sip of wine she just took, her eyes wide in surprise. Was he lying to impress her parents? *Why don't I know about any of this?*

All eyes shifted to her as she grabbed her cloth napkin and cleaned up the small splatter she had made on the tabletop.

"Ngozi, since you don't drink alcohol much, maybe you should take it easy on that wine," Valerie said.

Chance frowned deeply. "She drinks—"

Ngozi kicked his shin under the table, silencing him.

He grunted as he eyed her with a hard stare.

"You're right, Ma. I better stick to water," she said, setting the goblet of wine aside as she avoided Chance's confused stare.

Their conversation continued, and the air became less tense as the questioning of Chance subsided. Ngozi sat back and observed her parents and her man as the conversation switched to politics. She had *never* imagined introducing her parents to a man other than Dennis—and definitely assumed they would resent him because of their fondness of her deceased husband.

This isn't bad. Not bad at all.

"So how long have you been interested in my daughter?" Valerie asked, before sliding a bite of food in her mouth.

Ngozi sat up straight. *What now? Weren't they just talking about the president?*

"Not long, really," she said, purposefully vague.

Chance gave her another odd expression. "From the first day we met, I wanted to know more about her other than her beauty," he said, resting his eyes on Ngozi.

She swallowed a sudden lump in her throat, finding herself unable to look away from him.

"I have discovered that she is as brilliant, caring, empathetic, loyal and funny as she is beautiful," he added.

Her entire body warmed under his praise. It was hard to deny that in time she had not felt appreciated or respected in her marriage. It was as if the success in her career had to be diminished to soothe the ego of a man used to being in the lead.

With Chance, it was different. He was her biggest champion.

After dinner and some more polite conversation over coffee and drinks, Ngozi looked on as Chance shook her father's hand and offered her mother a polite hug. "It was good to meet you both," he said.

"Same here," her father said with a nod, turning his attention to his nightly ritual of smoking a cigar and reading the local newspaper, *The Passion Grove Press*, which was mostly news and tidbits about the small town and the achievements of its residents.

"See, I survived," Chance said as they walked together to the front door.

Ngozi nodded, wrapping both of her arms around one of his. "Yes, you did," she said, looking up at him.

At the sound of footsteps, she quickly released him, but relaxed when she turned to find Reeds carrying Chance's leather coat. "Thank you, Reeds," she said.

"No problem," he said, undraping it from over his arm and handing it to Chance with a warm smile. "Drive safe, sir."

"Thank you."

Ngozi looked up at Chance but was surprised by the troubled look clouding his handsome features. "What's wrong?"

"Nothing," he said, outstretching each arm to pull on his fur-lined coat to defeat the arctic northeaster snow still dominating the March weather. "Are you coming back to Alpine with me?"

Her hands paused in smoothing the collar of his coat. "No, not tonight."

"You haven't stayed over except that one time," he said, his brows dipping as he brought his own hands up to cover hers.

Ngozi forced a smile, remembering her parents' ambushing her that next morning. "I will again," she said, conciliating him.

"Not with me, Ngozi," he said. "No, ma'am. Save the show for those who purchased a ticket. Me? I want nothing but the real. So, no, not with me. Never with me."

Ngozi withdrew her hands from his and rubbed them together as she looked into his eyes. "You're the only one who makes me feel like I can be me, whatever that may be. Shit show and all," she said, moving to take a seat on the bottom of the staircase.

Chance walked over to stand in front of where she sat, his hands now pressed into the pockets of his coat.

"I just would prefer my parents not know we've... uh...we're...intimate," she said.

He frowned as he looked up at the large chandelier above their heads. "Or that you drink. Or how long we've been together. Or a dozen other things I saw you outright lie or skirt the truth around tonight," he said.

"Really, Chance?" she asked, leaning to the side a bit as she gave him a stare filled with attitude.

"Really," he affirmed, looking down at her. "It was quite a performance."

Ngozi rose and moved up two steps so they were eye level with each other. "Don't judge me, Chance," she warned.

"Like you did about the lawsuit?" he asked, his voice chiding.

Wow.

"I'm wrong for making sure I'm not wasting my time trying to build something with you?" she asked.

"No, definitely not. Just like it's okay for me to now be skeptical about moving forward after seeing you so willingly—and so easily—present yourself as whatever is needed in the moment," he countered.

"You don't trust me, Chance?" she asked, her feelings hurt by the thought of that.

He shook his head. "I didn't say that," he insisted.

"But I do wonder if you even trust yourself to be who and what you truly want to be, if you are so busy playing the role of Ms. Perfect."

Ngozi arched a brow. "That's not playing perfect—it's providing respect," she countered.

"And who were you respecting by staying in an unhappy marriage—"

Ngozi held up both hands with her palms facing him as she shook her head vigorously. "No, you don't get to focus on issues you think I have and ignore the emotional baggage sitting on your own doorstep."

They fell silent. The air was tense. Gone was the joy they usually had just being in each other's company.

"It seems we both have some stuff we need to fix," Chance finally offered.

She nodded in agreement. "Maybe we should work on that before trying to complicate each other's lives further," she said, unable to overlook her hurt and offense at his words.

He looked surprised, but then he nodded, as well. "Maybe," he agreed.

What are you doing, Ngozi? What are we doing?

She descended the few steps, moving beyond him to stride across the space to open the front door. The chilly winter winds instantly pushed inside. She trembled as goose bumps covered her.

Chance looked at her over his broad shoulder before he turned with a solemn expression and walked over to stand before her. "We never can seem to get this right," he said, wiping away a snowflake that blew in and landed on her cheek.

Ngozi had to fight not to lean into his touch. "Maybe one day we'll both be ready for this," she said, sadness filling her as she doubted the truth of it.

They had taken a chance on each other and failed.

"Maybe," Chance agreed.

With one final look shared between them, he turned and left.

Ngozi gave not one care about the brutal cold as she stood in the doorway and watched him walk out of her life at her request.

A warm hand touched her arm and pulled her back from the door to close it. She turned to find Reeds just as a tear raced down her cheek. Her feelings were not bruised because he had pointed out what she knew about herself—she flew under the radar in her personal life by putting on a facade to make everyone but herself happy. Having it presented to her on a platter by the man she loved had been embarrassing, but the true hurt was his inability to release Helena from his life and move on. That stung like crazy, and she'd be a fool to risk her heart when she wasn't sure his wasn't too bruised by another woman to love her in return.

"It's just a mess, Reeds," she admitted, wiping away her tears and blinking rapidly to prevent any more from rising and falling.

"You've been hiding your tears since your brother's death, Ngozi," he said, his wise eyes searching hers. "Shrinking yourself. Denying yourself. You were a child taking on the role and responsibility of an adult by trying to adjust her life for grown people. Now you're grown, and you're still doing it. And I'll tell you this—I'm glad *somebody* finally said it."

Ngozi was startled. "Say what now?" she asked.

"Listen, my job around here is to make sure the house operates well and the staff acts right. It's not to cross the line and interject myself between the people who pay me and their daughter whom I adore, but I will tell you this—since your young man opened the door. They feel they are protecting you just as much as you feel you're protecting them, and I think you're all wrong for the way you're going about it. Avoidance is never the answer."

And now Ngozi was confused, because she knew Reeds wouldn't speak on personal family matters—especially if he wasn't sure about his opinion.

"Well, since it's clear you overheard my conversation with Chance," she said, kicking into attorney mode, "why should I risk my heart for a man who won't let something go for me?"

Reeds smiled. "And if he did? If he readily agreed to drop this lawsuit you're so worried about, would you have been prepared in that moment to be the woman he is requesting of you—to stand up for yourself and demand your happiness in whatever way *you* see fit?"

Ngozi quickly shifted through emotions. *How could I love someone when I haven't learned to fully discover and love myself?*

"I believe you have just put me at a rare loss, Reeds," she admitted as he chuckled.

"Now that is high praise, Madam Counselor," he said, reaching over to squeeze her hand before he turned and walked away toward the dining room, presumably to ensure the staff had cleaned the area.

She crossed her arms over her chest and rubbed the back of her upper arms as she made her way back to the den. Her parents were lying on the sofa together watching television. Her eyes shifted to the spot on the floor in front of the polished entertainment center. An image of her and her brother, Haaziq, sitting cross-legged replayed in her mind. They were dressed in nightclothes and laughing at some TV comedy as their parents snuggled.

It was a memory that was hard to forget because of its regular occurrence in their life as a family.

In the image, he slowly faded away and she was left alone.

God, I miss my brother. I miss him so much.

"Ngozi? What's wrong?" her mother asked, rising from where she had been resting her head against her father's chest.

She smiled and shook her head, falling into her all-too-familiar role. "Nothing," she lied, sounding fine but feeling hollow.

"Okay," Valerie said, reclaiming her spot. "You had an odd look on your face."

And just like that, a hiccup in their life, a spot of imperfection, was corrected.

"Is your friend gone?" her father asked.

Maybe forever.

Ngozi nodded, feeling overwhelmed. *When do my feelings matter?*

"Mama," she called out, wringing her hands together.

Valerie looked over at her. "Yes?"

"I lied before," she admitted.

"About what?" her mother asked, rising from her husband's chest once more.

"I was thinking about…about…how we all sat in here every night, me, you, Daddy and… Haaziq, and watched TV before you would send us to bed," she admitted, wincing and releasing a harsh gasp as one tear and then another raced down her cheek. "And how much I miss him."

Her parents shared a long, knowing look before her mother rose to come over to her and her father used the iPad to turn off the television.

And at the first feel of her mother's arms wrapping around her body and embracing her, Ngozi buried her face in her neck and inhaled her familiar scent.

"We knew this was coming, we just didn't know it would take so long," her father added, coming close to massage warm circles on her back.

Ngozi enjoyed the warmth of their comfort, and cried like she had never cried before.

Chapter 9

Three months later

Chance leaned against the wall of the hospital with his hands pressed deep into the pockets of the dark denim he wore. As hospital personnel moved past him in completion of their duties and he ignored the scent of illness and antiseptic blending in the air, Chance eyed room 317.

On the other side of the closed door was his father. Jeffrey Castillo.

He'd never seen him. Never met him. Never known anything about him except he was his father.

Over the last ninety days, he had made his life one adventure after another. Helicopter skiing in Alaska. Diving with sharks on the Australian coast off a megayacht. Shopping at the House of Bijan in

Beverly Hills. Kayaking in Norway. Watching the grand prix in Monte Carlo. Skydiving in Dubai.

And then he'd received an inbox message on Facebook from a woman introducing herself as his father's wife and letting him know his father was terminally ill and wanted to finally meet his eldest son. That was the day before, and now here he was. Chance hadn't even told his mother.

I don't know why I'm here.

Pushing up off the wall, he walked down the length of the corridor to the window, looking out at the cars lined up in the many parking spots and at the traffic whizzing past on the street.

He froze when he spotted a tall dark-skinned woman climb from a red car and make her way toward the hospital's main entrance. His gut clenched until the moment he realized she was not Ngozi.

"Chance?"

He turned from the window to find a pretty round-faced woman with a short silvery hairdo paused at the door to his father's hospital room. It was his father's wife, Maria. She gave him a warm smile as she walked up to him.

"You came," she said.

"I haven't gone in," he admitted.

Her eyes showed her understanding of his hesitation. "If you decide not to, I won't tell him," she said. "The man he is today is not the man he was before. Life has caused him to change, but that will never top how you must have felt growing up without his presence in your life."

Chance liked her. Empathy was always a bridge to understanding and respect.

"Does he know you reached out to me?" he asked, looking down the length of the hall to the closed door.

She shook her head. "No, I didn't want to disappoint him if you—or the others—chose not to come."

Chance went still with a frown. "Others?"

Maria nodded, bending her head to look down as she opened her purse and removed a folded, well-worn envelope with frayed edges. She pressed it into his hands.

Chance allowed his body to lean against the wall as he took in the list of three names in faded ink—his and two more. "And these are?" he asked, looking at the woman.

"Your two brothers," she said, offering him a gentle smile.

Chance deeply frowned. When he was younger, he was optimistic enough to wonder if he had sisters and brothers. Age and the passing of time with no such knowledge had led to him not caring and then not wondering about it all.

"Jeffrey and I also have a daughter, Chance," she said gently. "Her name is Camila."

His father. A stepmother. And three half siblings.

Chance shook his head, not quite sure of anyone's intention and whether he was ready for a new family. "I need time," he admitted, folding and shoving the envelope in his back pocket.

"I understand," Maria said. "Please keep in mind that your fath—that Jeffrey is very ill, and this may be your last opportunity to see him alive."

He nodded as his emotions whirled around like a tornado.

"Ma?"

He looked down the hall at a tall, slender woman in her midtwenties, with short jet-black hair and a shortbread complexion, standing in the open doorway to room 317. He knew from the lean beauty of her face and the similarities in their look that she was his sister, Camila. Camila Castillo.

"I'm coming," Maria said, giving him one more smile filled with her desire for him to meet his father before she turned and walked to her daughter.

"Who is that?" Camila asked, swiping her long bangs out of her face as she eyed him in open curiosity.

"Someone who knows your father," Maria said, offering a hint at the truth but successfully evading it.

Both women gave him one final look before entering the hospital room and closing the door behind them.

Quickly, Chance strode down the middle of the hallway, his height and strength seeming to make the space smaller. He felt pressure filling his chest as he pressed the button for the elevator with far more vigor than necessary. Coming there had become more than he bargained for. Once on the elevator, he pulled the frayed envelope from his back pocket and lightly rubbed the side of his thumb against the faded block lettering that he assumed to be that of his father.

A name on an envelope wasn't much, but it was more of a thought than he'd ever imagined his father to have spent on him.

Chance stopped the elevator doors from closing

and stepped off, making his way back down the hall
to room 317. The door opened, and Camila exited. He
stepped out of her path, but she stood there looking
up at him even as the door closed behind her. "Excuse
me," he said, moving to step past her.

"You look just like my father. Are we related?"
she asked in Spanish.

Chance froze and then stepped back, causing a
nurse to have to swerve to avoid bumping into him.
"My bad," he apologized.

The pretty blonde gave him an appreciative look.
"No problem," she stressed before continuing on her
way with a look back at him over her shoulder.

The door opened again, and Chance's eyes landed
on the gray-haired man lying on the hospital bed. He
had but a brief glimpse as the door closed. He was
surprised his heart pounded with such vigor.

Maria eyed Chance and then her daughter.

"Camila, I thought you went down to the café," she
said, reaching to press a folded bill into the younger
woman's hand. "Bring me something sweet to nib-
ble on."

"But, Ma—"

"Adios, Camila," Maria said, gently nudging her
daughter on her way.

With one last long look at Chance, she turned and
walked down the hall to the elevators.

"You came back," Maria said, squeezing his hand.
"Come, Chance. Come."

Gently, he withdrew his hand, but he followed her
into the room.

"Mi amor, mi amor," she said gently in a singsong fashion. "Look who is here, *mi amor*. It is Chance, your son."

Chance stood at the foot of the bed and looked at the tall and thin man whose gaunt features could not deflect that he looked like a younger, fuller version of his father. Jeffrey opened his eyes. They were slightly tinged with yellow and glassy, but he couldn't deny when they filled with tears.

Jeffrey reached out his hand to Chance and bent his fingers, beckoning him.

For so long, when he was younger, he wondered about the moment he would meet his father. Never had he imagined it happening on his deathbed with cancer winning in the fight for his life. His hesitation was clear as Maria eyed him and then her husband. His father's hand dropped some, as if the effort exhausted him.

That evoked compassion from him, and Chance moved to the side of the bed to take his father's hand in his own. His grip lacked strength. The scent of oncoming death clung to the air around him.

"Forgive me," Jeffrey said, his Spanish accent present even in the weakened state of his tone.

Chance remained stoic even as he looked down into his father's face. He didn't know if his heart could soften to him. His mother had worked double shifts to make up for the help she did not receive from him. Even now, he didn't know if she would feel betrayed by his coming to his father's bedside.

"Forgive me?" Jeffrey asked this time.

Chance glanced across the bed to find Maria had

quietly left them alone in the room. He shifted his gaze back down to his father. It was amazing that he could look so much like a man he had never met. His imprint was undeniable.

Chance released a breath and looked up at the ceiling as the emotions from his childhood came flooding back to him. He clenched his jaw.

The grip on his hand tightened.

Chance looked down. "Why?" he asked.

Jeffrey squeezed his eyes shut, and tears fell as he shook his head.

Chance hoped to be a father one day. He knew he would do better than his own sire because he would be present, scolding when needed and loving always, but *if* he made a misstep, he would hope on his deathbed he would be forgiven. He believed you had to give what you hoped to receive for yourself.

"Te perdono," Chance said, offering this stranger the clemency he requested.

His father pulled his hand to his mouth to kiss the back of it and then made the sign of the cross as he gripped it. *"Gracias,"* he whispered up to him.

He had learned through the loss of the woman he loved that vengeance was a drawback he refused to let hinder his life again.

Passion Grove was truly home.

Ngozi adjusted the large oil painting she'd hung above her fireplace and then stood back to observe her handiwork. The artwork was alive with the vibrant colors and matched the decor of her new home in the affluent small town. It was a rental, but the Realtor said the owners may be interested in selling the four-bedroom, four-bathroom Colonial early next year.

Regardless, for the last month it was home.

"When did you get so Afrocentric?"

Ngozi sighed at the sound of her mother's voice behind her. "I don't know, Ma, maybe my name inspired me," she said as she turned and eased her hand into the pockets of her oversize coveralls.

Her father chuckled from his spot relaxing on her bright red leather sofa.

Valerie gave him a sharp eye that only made him laugh harder. "With the new hair and all this artwork everywhere, you really are taking us back to the motherland," she said, touching a large wooden African ceremonial mask that hung on the wall by the door.

Ngozi touched her faux locks, which were twisted up into a topknot. "My house, my way, Ma," she said, coming close to kiss her cheek before moving past her to close the French doors and unfortunately cut off the breeze of April air drifting in from outside.

"You know, this new and improved Ngozi is a lot chattier," Valerie said.

"Well, I like it," Horace said, rising from the sofa.

"Me, too, Dad," Ngozi agreed, looking around at the spacious family room, which had been the last of the areas she decorated.

For the first time in a long time, longer than she could remember, Ngozi had the same confidence and tenacity that made her a conqueror in the courtroom in her personal life. She enjoyed living her life by her gut instincts and not just by what she thought others wanted her to do or to be. Not living to please others was freeing.

Her parents, particularly her mother, were adjusting to discovering just who their daughter truly was.

Valerie winked at Ngozi. "If you like it, I love it," she said.

Ngozi had discovered over the last ninety days that her parents weren't as strict and judgmental as she'd thought growing up. She'd never felt so close to them.

The night she'd opened up about Haaziq, they'd discussed the impact of his death on their lives. She'd discovered that they tiptoed around her just as much as she placated them. In the end, they were a family trying to cope with a death and just didn't know how to do it.

Now if a memory of Haaziq rose, no one shied away from the thought, and instead they would share a laugh or just reminisce on the time they did get to have him in their lives. And if they were moved to a few tears, that was fine. They grieved him and got through the moment.

"Horace, you ready?" Valerie asked, reaching for her designer tote bag sitting on one of the round end tables flanking the leather sofa. "The town council is cutting the ribbon on the Spring Bazaar, and I do not want to be late."

He eyed his wife as she smoothed her white-gloved hands over the skirt of the pale apricot floral lace dress she wore. It was beautiful and fit her frame well, but it was completely over the top for a local bazaar being held on the grounds of the middle school that offered the works of artists and crafters with plenty of vendors, good food, rides and live music.

"Has she always been so extra?" Ngozi whispered to her dad as her mother reapplied her sheer coral lip gloss.

"Yes, and I love every bit of it," he said with warm appreciation in his tone.

Ngozi looked at him, clearly a man still enthralled by his wife.

I want someone to look at me that way.

Not someone. Chance.

Ngozi pushed thoughts of him away.

"I never wanted to marry until I met and eventually fell in love with your mother," Horace said, walking over to wrap his arm around his wife's waist and pull her close. They began to sway together as they looked into each other's eyes.

"Right," Valerie agreed. "And I was so career driven that at thirty-nine I began to assume I would never find love and have a family of my own...until your daddy put on the full-court press for my attention. I never assumed this man I competed with in the courtroom for so many years would turn into the love of my life."

"Same here," he agreed, doing a little shimmy and leading them into a spin.

"I tamed that dog," she teased.

"The dog tamed himself," he countered.

"So I guess your always loving that Vincent and

Associates Law also spells out VAL isn't proof enough that you're sprung?" Valerie stroked his nape.

"And you're not?" he asked, with a little jerk that pulled her body closer.

They shared an intimate, knowing laugh.

"Respect your elders, Horace," she said. "You're lucky I don't make you call me Mrs. Vincent."

"Two whole years older than me. Big deal," he said.

Ngozi looked at them with pleasure at their happiness and a bit of melancholy that she didn't have that, as well.

Her parents were in their early seventies but lived life—and looked—as if they were far younger.

"You're going to wrinkle my dress, Horace," Valerie said, not truly sounding as if she cared.

"Wait until you see what I do to it when I get you home," he said low in his throat before nuzzling his face against her neck.

Ngozi rolled her eyed. "*Hellllllooo*, I'm still here. Daughter in the room," she said.

"And? How you think you got here, little girl?" Valerie asked, ending their dance with a kiss that cleared her lips of the gloss she'd just applied. "Your conception was *not* immaculate."

"But it was spectacular," Horace said.

"Don't you make us late," she said in playful warning.

Ngozi walked across the spacious family room. "Okay, let me help mosey y'all along," she said over her shoulder as she left the room and crossed the foyer to open the front door.

They followed behind her.

"Any chance you're going to change?" Valerie asked, eying the overalls.

In the past, Ngozi would have found a pretty spring dress to wear to please her mother, complete with pearls and a cardigan. "No, ma'am."

"Leave her be, Val," Horace said before leaving the house and taking the stairs down to his silver two-door Rolls Royce Wraith sitting on the paved drive.

Valerie quietly made prayer hands in supplication as she left.

"See you later at the bazaar, Ma," Ngozi said, closing the door.

She turned and leaned against it, looking at her home. She was proud she had taken a large space and infused it with warmth and color. Not even the apartment she'd shared with her husband had her personal touch. She had chosen what she thought he would like.

No, this is all me.

Ngozi closed her eyes and just enjoyed being in her own place and her own space for the first time in her life.

Ding-dong.

The doorbell startled her. Ngozi's heartbeat was racing as she turned to open the door. She smiled at Josh, one of the high school kids who served as deliverymen for The Gourmet Way, the grocery store on Main Street that specialized in delicacies.

"Hello, Ms. Johns, I have your weekly delivery," the tall freckle-faced blond said with a smile that showed off his Invisalign braces.

"Come on in," she said, closing the door when he obeyed and then leading him with the heavy black basket he carried through the family room, which opened into the gourmet kitchen.

Josh set the basket on top of the marble island.

"Are you going to the Spring Bazaar?" Ngozi asked as she removed a twenty-dollar bill from the billfold sitting with files and her laptop on the large kitchen table before the open French doors.

"As soon as my shift is over," he said, accepting the tip with a polite nod.

"See you there," she offered as he turned to leave.

"Bye, Ms. Johns."

Ngozi opened the basket and removed the perishables to place in her fridge or freezer, deciding to leave the little things like chutneys, a canister of caviar, bottles of cordials and black garlic. She did allow herself a treat of thinly sliced *soppressata*, broke a small piece off the ball of fresh mozzarella and wrapped both around a garlic-stuffed olive.

"Vegan who?" she said before taking a bite.

Mmm.

After popping the last bite into her mouth, she cleaned her moist fingertips on a napkin before reclaiming her seat at the table. She had an office upstairs in one of the spare bedrooms, but the light was the brightest and the breeze from outside the best at the kitchen table. It was Saturday, but she had a court case to prepare for in defense of an heir charged with murdering his parents.

The Skype incoming-call tone sounded from her tablet.

Ngozi eyed it, reaching over the open files with pen in hand to tap the screen and accept the video, then propping the tablet up by its case. She laughed as her goddaughter's face filled the screen and she released a spit bubble that exploded. "Hello, Aliyah," she cooed.

"Hewwoo, Godmommy!"

Ngozi arched a brow. "Really, Alessandra, I thought you were a co-CEO of a billion-dollar corporation, not offering voice characterizations for the cutest baby in the world," she drawled.

Alessandra sat Aliyah on her lap in her office and smiled into the screen over the top of her reading glasses. "I do both. I'm complex," she said with a one-shoulder shrug.

"A woman's worth," Ngozi said.

"Right…although Alek is pretty hands-on with her. I can't really complain. In the boardroom, bedroom and nursery, we are getting the job done together."

"Why can't we all be that lucky?" Ngozi said wistfully.

"*We* all could," Alessandra said with a pointed look.

Chance.

Her friend had thankfully agreed not to mention him, but it was clear from the way Alessandra stopped that his name almost tumbled from her lips.

Ngozi looked out the window at the trees neatly

surrounding the backyard without really seeing them. At a different time in their lives, what they shared could have blossomed into that lifetime of love her parents had. She smiled at the thought of Chance— older, wiser and more handsome—lovingly teasing her as they danced to their music no one else heard.

"I thought we could ride to the bazaar together," Alessandra offered.

"I'll probably walk. The school isn't that far from here," she said.

"Alek and Naim, his brother, are in London on business…so you won't be third-wheeling, as you call it."

Ngozi smiled.

"I'm on the way."

She ended the Skype call and rose to close the French doors before she grabbed her wallet and bill-fold. She dropped those items into the bright orange designer tote bag sitting on the half-moon table by the door. She used the half bath off the foyer to freshen up before sliding her feet into leather wedges and applying bright red lip gloss.

On the security screen, she saw the black 1954 Jaguar MK VII sedan that had belonged to Alessandra's father. Ngozi slid her tote onto the crook of her arm and left the house. Roje, Alessandra's driver, climbed from the car. The middle-aged man with a smooth bald head and silvery goatee looked smart and fit in his black button-up shirt and slacks as he left the car to open the rear door for her.

The scent of his cologne was nice, and Ngozi bit

back a smile as she remembered the private moments he had shared with Alessandra's mother-in-law. She could easily see how the man was hard for LuLu to resist.

"Thank you," Ngozi said to him before climbing in the rear of the car beside Aliyah's car seat.

"Soo...does Alek know about his mother and your driver?" Ngozi asked as she allowed six-month-old Aliyah to grip her index finger.

Alessandra gasped in surprise.

Ngozi gave her friend a look that said *deny it.*

"I plead the fifth."

"You can plead whatever. I *know* what I saw," Ngozi said, eyeing Roje coming around the front of the vintage car through the windshield mirror.

"What?" Alessandra asked.

Aliyah cooed as if she, too, was curious.

"You tell what you know, and I'll tell what I know. Then *we'll* keep their secret," she said.

Roje climbed into the driver's seat and eyed the women in the rearview mirror before starting the car. "Ready?" he asked, his voice deep and rich.

They both nodded and gave him a smile.

Roje eyed them oddly before pulling off down the driveway.

They rode in silence until they reached Passion Grove Middle, a stately brick building with beautiful ivy topiaries and a large playground surrounded by wrought iron finish with scrollwork. Like most community events in the small town, attendance was high, with those from neighboring cities attending the annual affair, as well.

"The elusive Lance Millner is doing a book signing?" Ngozi asked after reading the large sign as Roje pulled the car to a stop before the open gate.

"That's a first around here," Alessandra said.

"Hell, I have never seen him without that damn hat on," Ngozi said. "I have got to see this."

"Ladies, you go in and I'll search for some parking on the street," Roje said, climbing from the driver's seat to open the rear door and then retrieve the folded stroller.

"Good idea. Thanks," Alessandra said, unsnapping Aliyah from her car seat.

Ngozi climbed from the car and looked at the crowd milling around the artwork and crafts on display, the vendors selling their wares, food trucks offering tasty treats, live music offering entertainment, and a few carnival rides on the athletic fields for the children.

"Roje, I'm sure you don't want to hang around for this, so you can go and come back for us in a few," Alessandra said.

Ngozi turned just as Roje smiled and inclined his head in agreement.

"I would like to run a quick errand," he admitted.

"To Manhattan?" Alessandra asked.

LuLu Ansah lived in a beautiful penthouse apartment on the upper east side.

Roje's expression was curious as he pulled mirror shades from the front pocket of his shirt and slid them on his face. "Would you like me to pick up something for you in the city?" he asked, sidestepping her question.

"A little happiness for yourself," Alessandra said.

"I wish," he admitted. "Sometimes life gets in the way."

Ngozi thought of Chance. Her love had not been enough to stop life from getting in their way.

Chance sat on his private plane, looking out the window at the clouds seeming to fade as darkness descended. In the two weeks since he'd met his father, he hadn't returned to see him again. Instead, he had continued his tour around the world. Paris. London. China. And now he was headed to his estate in Cabrera.

He pulled his wallet from his back pocket and opened it to remove the well-worn envelope.

More than anything, it was his siblings he was avoiding. He wasn't ready. Chance was well aware that he was a man of considerable means, and he had no idea what Pandora's box of problems he was setting himself up for with the inclusion of so many new people in his life. Suddenly. And perhaps suspiciously.

Was his father's sudden need for reconciliation more about his guilt as death neared, or his discovery of his sudden billionaire status?

I'd be a fool not to consider that.

He was just as aware he was in a position to help people who were his family by default. By blood.

I'd be an asshole not to consider that.

Chance put the envelope back in its safe spot inside his wallet before rising from his ergonomic reclining chair to walk to his bedroom suite. He was exhausted from his quests and ready to settle down in one spot to rest and relax. Nothing spoke more of relaxation to him than being on his estate in Cabrera.

Except making love to Ngozi.

He thought of her. Moments they had shared in fun or in sex. Her smile. Her scent. Her touch.

Damn. When will I get over her?

He flopped over onto his back and unlocked his iPhone to pull up a picture of her in his bed, her body covered by a sheet as she playfully stuck her tongue out at him.

When will my love go away?

He deleted the picture and dropped his phone onto the bed, wishing like hell it was that easy to erase her from his thoughts and his heart.

"Congratulations on another win, Ngozi."

"Do you even know what an L is?"

"Congrats."

"Ngozi, good win."

"District attorneys hate to see you coming, Counselor."

Ngozi kept her facade cool, like it was just another day at work, accepting each bit of praise as she made her way through the offices of Vincent and Associates Law. She smiled, thinking of her parents' inside joke about the acronym. This was the house Horace

Vincent had built, and his love for his wife was in the name.

And now I'm making my mark.

Instead of heading to her office, Ngozi turned and rode the elevator up one story to the executive offices of the senior partners. "Good afternoon, Ms. Johns," the receptionist for the senior partners greeted her.

"Good afternoon, Evelyn," she said, always making sure in her years at the firm to know the name of each staff member.

To her, that was one of the true signs of leadership.

"Can I get anything for you?" Evelyn asked.

"Not a thing but thank you. I just want to hang out in my dad's office for a little bit," she said softly, moving past the reception desk.

"Actually, he's in today."

Ngozi paused and looked back at her in surprise. "Really?" she said, unsure why she suddenly felt nervous.

Evelyn nodded before turning her attention to the ringing phone.

Large executive offices were arranged in a horseshoe pattern around the reception area, but it was the office dominating the rear wall of the floor toward which she walked. Her briefcase lightly slapped against the side of her leg in the silk oxblood suit she wore with matching heels. Reaching the white double doors, she knocked twice before opening the door.

"Getting my office ready for me, Pops?" she quipped, but the rest of her words faded as all five managing partners of Vincent and Associates Law turned to eye her.

Ngozi dropped her head abashedly. "My apologies, I thought my father was here alone," she said, moving forward to offer her hand to each partner.

"It will be yours one day, Ngozi," her father said as she came to stand beside his desk. "Just as soon as you're ready."

She nodded in agreement. Her father offered her no shortcuts to success, and she never expected any. She would become the principal partner of the firm her father started by consistent wins and proven leadership, bringing in high-level clients with strong billable hours. She was just thirty, and although she was making good headway, she had a long journey ahead of her.

Ngozi didn't want it any other way.

"More wins like today definitely doesn't hurt," Angela Brinks, a sharp and decisive blonde in her early sixties, offered.

"Thank you," Ngozi said, holding her briefcase in front of her. "It was a tough acquittal, but my staff pulled it out and the client is heavily considering moving some other corporate business our direction."

"I understand you played a role in Chance Castillo putting VAL on retainer to oversee his corporate and business matters," Greg Landon said.

Chance.

Her heart seemed to pound against her chest.

She hadn't known that. She made it her business to avoid even discovering the outcome of his case.

"Everything okay?" her father asked.

Get it together, Ngozi.

"Yes," she said. "Actually, I'm going to leave you all to the meeting I interrupted. I actually have another case to prep."

"Federal, right?" Monique Reeves asked. She was the newest managing partner—and the youngest, at forty-five.

Ngozi found the woman smart, formidable and tenacious—her role model, particularly as an African American woman.

"I would offer you my expertise in that arena… but I don't think you need it. Still, the offer is on the table," Monique said.

"Thank you, Monique, that's good to know," she said before moving toward the door. "Have a good day, everyone."

As soon as she exited and closed the door, Ngozi dropped onto the long leather bench against the wall, letting her briefcase land on the floor as she pressed one hand to the side of her face and the other against her racing heart.

Chance. Chance. Chance.

Just when she had a nearly complete day without his invading her thoughts and creating a craving… BOOM! Nearly four months since their breakup and she was not over him.

Not yet.

Ngozi cleared her throat and stood with her briefcase in hand as she stiffened her back and notched her chin a bit higher, then made her way down the long length of the hall.

But I will be...one day.

I hope.

Chapter 10

One month later

Ngozi brought her swift run to an end as she came to Main Street of Passion Grove. She released puffs of air through pursed lips and checked her vitals and mileage via her Fitbit. She waved and smiled to those townspeople she knew as she continued to move her feet in place while she waited for her heart rate to gradually decline.

Feeling thirsty, she walked down the block toward the bakery, pausing a moment at the display in the window of the high-end boutique, Spree, that offered the latest trend in designer clothing. A beautiful silver beaded sheath dress with a short hem caught her eye, and she knew if she wasn't still sweaty and hot from a run, she would have gone into the boutique to try it on. "Another time," she promised herself, continuing on her way.

The large black metal bell sounded as she opened the door to La Boulangerie. The scent of fresh-brewed coffee and decadent sweets filled the air. There was a small line of customers awaiting treats in the pastry shop decorated like old-world Europe, with modern accents and brick walls. It was a warm Saturday in June, and the townspeople were out and about, milling around their small downtown area.

She checked incoming messages on her phone as she waited her turn. Soft hairs seemed to tickle her nape and she kept smoothing them with her free hand, also aware that she suddenly felt a nervousness that made her wonder if she'd caught a flu bug or something. When the hairs stood on end, she turned but didn't recognize any of the people in line behind her.

"Welcome to La Boulangerie. How may I help you?"

Ngozi faced forward. Her eyes widened to see Alessandra's cousin and her former client behind the counter. "Marisa, you work here?" she asked, her surprise clear.

Alessandra's family, the Dalmounts, was a super-rich family of prominence. She doubted her salary matched the weekly stipend Alessandra allotted her entire family, following the tradition her father had started when he was the head of the family.

Marisa, a beautiful young woman in her late twenties with a massive head full of natural curls that rested on her petite shoulders, smiled and shrugged one shoulder. "I've never had a job and I have to start somewhere," she said, her voice soft and raspy as if she could bring true justice to a soulful song. Although Ngozi recalled that her deceased father was Mexican, there was no hint of a Spanish accent.

"That's true, but I'm surprised Alessandra couldn't get you something entry level at ADG," Ngozi said, taking a small step back to eye the desserts on display in the glass case.

"I'm just starting to think a handout from your rich family isn't the best way for me," she said, sounding vague.

"Not many young women would feel that way," Ngozi said, pushing aside her curiosity. "I'm proud of you," she offered, feeling odd giving praise to a woman not far from her own age.

"Thanks," Marisa said.

"Hey, Bill," Ngozi said, smiling at the man with shoulder-length blond hair pulled back in a ponytail. As always, his black apron with Bill the Pâtissier embroidered on it was in place.

"Afternoon," he said, his tone appreciative as he gave her a slow once-over in her pink form-fitting running gear.

Bill wants some chocolate in his life.

"Marisa, I'll take a bottle of water and a fresh fruit cup for my walk home," she said, politely ignoring his flirty look. She was used to it. Bill had long ago let his intentions be known, and she had always turned him down gently.

He just chuckled at her deflection before heading back to the rear of the bakery.

"Coming right up," Marisa said, using the back of her hand to swipe away a long tendril that escaped from her top knot before pulling on gloves.

Ngozi was tempted to purchase a mini walnut Danish ring, able to tell it was packed with cinnamon sugar. She wasn't ever going vegan, but she did try to fit in healthy eating when she could. *Still...that Danish is looking like a treat.*

"Let me get a walnut Danish ring, too," she said, pulling her credit card from the zippered pocket on the sleeve of her running jacket.

Marisa gave her a knowing smile as she used tongs to slide the treat into a small brown paper bag with the bakery's logo. She took the card and handed Ngozi her treats and a small foil packet with a wet wipe for her hands. Soon she returned with her receipt. "Thank you and come again," she said.

"Bye, Marisa. I will," Ngozi said, turning away with a smile.

She tucked the water bottle under her arm and the Danish in her pocket before opening the wet wipe packet to wipe her hands.

"Ngozi."

Her body froze, but her heart raced a marathon, and those hairs on her nape stood on end. Now the nervous energy was familiar.

Chance.

Turning toward his voice, she spotted him sitting at a bistro table in the corner of the pastry shop with Alek. She hadn't even noticed them there. Chance unbent his tall frame—his tall, well-proportioned, strong frame—and waved an inviting hand to an empty chair across from him.

Ngozi hesitated.

They had done so well avoiding each other for all these months. And now, just like that, out of the clear blue sky, here they were.

Fate?

Perhaps.

Finally, she moved toward him, and it was as if everything else in the bakery outside of her line of vision on him blurred. With every step that brought her closer to him, her nerves felt more and more frayed.

Alek tossed the last of his powdered doughnut into his mouth before wiping his hands with a napkin and rising. "Good to see you, Ngozi," he said.

She just nodded, never taking her eyes off Chance.

Alek looked between his friend and his wife's best friend before walking out of the pastry shop as if he knew his presence was suddenly forgotten.

Chance reached around her to pull the chair out.

"Still the gentleman," she said, offering him a polite smile before she sat down and crossed one leg over the other.

"Of course, of course," Chance said, offering her a charming smile as he sat back down.

Ngozi set her water and the plastic container of fruit on the table as she eyed how good he looked in a navy tracksuit with one of his dozen or so Patek watches on his wrist. "You look good, Chance," she admitted, picking up the bottle to open and take a sip.

"So do you," he said, eyeing her before shifting his gaze out the window of the storefront.

They both fell silent.

Then they spoke at once.

"Ngozi—"

"Chance—"

They laughed.

"Our goddaughter is growing up fast," Ngozi said, searching for a neutral topic.

Chance nodded. "I got her a baby Lambo car. She'll be driving around their courtyard in no time."

"Only you would buy a baby a mini-Lambo," she said. "Is it pink or bright red?"

His smile widened. "Fire red, of course."

"Of course," she agreed.

More silence.

So many questions were sitting on the tip of her tongue, ready to tumble out.

"You're still running?" Chance asked.

Ngozi looked pensive. "Running from what?" she asked, instantly nervous an argument would ensue.

Chance shook his head. "No, I meant running. Exercising. Jogging," he said, making back-and-forth motions with his fists as if he were running.

"Oh," Ngozi said. "My bad. Yeah. I'm still running, addicted to the high of it. You?"

He nodded. "I did ten miles this morning," he said.

"I did like five around the lake and then came here for a little snack before I head back to my house," she said.

"Your house?" he asked.

Their eyes met.

Ngozi looked away first, opening the container to pop a grape into her mouth. "I moved out of my parents'," she said, lifting the container toward him in offering.

He picked it up and poured a few grapes into his hand. "How is it?"

"The house?" she asked.

"Living alone for the first time."

They shared another look.

"Necessary," she admitted. "It was time to trust myself to be who and what I truly want to be. Right?"

Those were the words he had given to her that night they'd ended their relationship. She could tell he caught the reference instantly.

"I only wanted the best for you," he explained.

Ngozi leaned forward to grasp his hand atop the table. "No, I'm not throwing shade. I needed to learn to want the best for me, too," she said.

He looked down at their hands clasped together and stroked her thumb with his.

Ngozi shivered, feeling a rush she could only guess was like an addict getting their first hit of drugs after a long break of sobriety. Not wanting to stir up the desire for him for which she was still in recovery, Ngozi gently withdrew her hand.

Chance instantly felt the loss of her touch. He looked down at his empty hand for a few beats before closing it into a fist.

He hadn't expected to run into Ngozi today. Even

with sharing godparent duties for baby Aliyah and each of their best friends being married to each other, they hadn't crossed paths. When she walked into the bakery, he'd watched her, but he wasn't even sure he wanted to make his presence known to her. They had moved on from each other. Survived the breakup.

He was so intent on letting her go about her day that he never let Alek, who had his back to the door, know that she was there. But he never lost sight of her. Never took his attention off her. He couldn't deny that he was pleased to see her again. And the jealousy sparked by Bill the Surfing Dude flirting with her could not be denied.

And when she reached for the door handle to leave, he had to stop her.

Now she pulled away from his touch.

"I saw they did a news story on your pro bono work," he offered, shifting away from sensitive subjects.

Ngozi nodded. "Recently, I've been doing more of that, but I think it's necessary. Not everyone is as privileged as we are to afford proper legal representation."

"People forget I grew up in the hood, but I have never forgotten, and I remember young dudes getting locked up for small crimes but staying in jail for months or longer because no one could afford bail or owned property to put up as collateral," he said.

"Maybe you could donate to help the underserved with that issue," Ngozi offered, tearing the label off the water bottle. "I'm thinking of setting up a nonprofit to do just that."

Nervous?

The thought that he still affected her made him anxious.

"Yes, or you could refer such cases to Second Chances, the nonprofit I've already set up to do that," he said, remembering all of her urgings for him to give back more with his wealth.

Remember, to whom much is given, much is required, Chance. God didn't bless you so that you can buy thousand-dollar burgers and million-dollar cars.

She looked taken aback. He gave her a wide smile, enjoying it. "Growth," he pointed out.

"Right," she agreed. "I will definitely send some referrals your way. Maybe I could talk to the partners about making an annual donation. It would be a good look for the firm."

Chance looked around the busy little pastry shop to avoid getting lost in her deep eyes. "So, we're teaming up?" he asked.

"For a noble cause? Definitely," she said without hesitation.

His heart hammered, and he could hardly believe that this woman still had the power to weaken him at the knees. "And more?" he asked.

Now, that caused her to noticeably pause.

"You know what, forget it," he said, shifting in his seat as he took a sip of the cup of Brazilian coffee he'd purchased. "You may have met someone."

"I haven't."

He cut his eyes up at her over the rim of his black cup. She didn't look away.

Chance set the cup down as he wrestled with the myriad feelings now swirling inside him, creating their own little storm.

"Have you?" she asked, her voice soft.

He shook his head. "How could I? When I *love* you, Ngozi," he confessed.

Her eyes widened, and she covered her mouth with her hand that trembled.

"I dropped the lawsuit when I realized that not having you in my life hurt far more than losing a million damn dollars on a stupid wedding I shouldn't be having anyway because she was *not* the love of my life," he said with such passion, leaning forward to take her free hand in his.

"You are, Ngozi. You are the love of *my* life."

Her grip tightened around his hand.

"I have tried to forget. Tried to move on. Tried not to dream about you. Tried like hell not to miss you. And until I saw you today, I convinced myself that I succeeded, but I didn't," he said, licking his suddenly dry mouth as his breaths quickened. He pressed a hand to his chest over his pounding heart, patting it. "You are in here. All of it. And I don't know what to do but love you. To have you. To fight for you. To take care of you. To make love to you. To be happier than I have ever been…with you."

Again, she tugged her hand, freeing it of his clasp as she rose, gathered her items and strode away.

His heart ached at her denial of his love. He clenched

his jaw and curled his fingers into a fist to fight the regret that filled him as he watched her walk away from him. She tossed the water bottle and the fruit cup in the trash can before walking back over.

He stiffened his spine and cleared his throat, preparing for another of their epic arguments—those he did not miss. *Especially in public.*

"Let's go," Ngozi said, extending her hand.

His confusion showed on his face. "Where?"

"To my house, to show you just how much I *love* you, Chance Castillo," she said with a sassy and tiny bite of her bottom lip.

His desire stirred in an instant.

As he grabbed his keys and took her hand to follow her, he was thankful that his heated blood didn't rush to his groin and leave him to walk out of the shop with a noticeable hard-on.

They barely made it through the front door.

Ngozi gasped as Chance pressed her body against it with his, holding her face with his hands as he kissed her with unrelenting passion that left her breathless and panting. And when he lowered his body against hers, layering her with hot kisses to her neck and the soft cleavage he revealed as he unzipped her jacket, she spread her arms and foolishly tried to grasp the wood of the door, looking for something to cling to as her hunger for him sent her reeling.

With each press of his lips or lick of his tongue against her skin—the valley of her breasts in her lace sports bra, her navel, the soft skin just above the edge of her undies—she lost a bit of sanity.

And cared not one bit.

Chance stripped her free of her clothing and her undergarments, leaving her naked and exposed to his eyes and his pleasure. And he enjoyed her long neck, rounded shoulders, long limbs, both pert breasts with large areolae surrounding her hard nipples and clean-shaven vulva with plump lips that only hinted at the pleasures it concealed.

With his hard and long erection pressing against the soft material of his pants, Chance hoisted Ngozi's naked body against his and carried her the short distance to the stairs, laying her on the steps and then spreading her smooth thighs as he knelt between them.

"I'm sweaty," she protested, pressing a hand to his forehead when he dipped his head above her core.

Chance looked up at her. "I don't give a good goddamn," he said low in his throat before brushing her hand away and dipping his head to lightly lick and then suck her warm fleshy bud.

He ached at the feel of it pulsing against his tongue, and when she cried out, arching her hips up off the steps as she shifted her hands to the back of his head, he sucked a little harder. Feeling heady from the scent and taste of her, Chance stroked inside her with his tongue.

"Chance," she gasped, her thighs snapping closed on his shoulders as she tried to fight off the pleasure.

He shook his head, denying her, not caring if he pushed her over the brink into insanity as he pressed her legs back open and continued his passionate on-slaught with a deep guttural moan.

"Please...please," she gasped.

He raised his head, his eyes intense as he took in hers brimming with pleasure, and her mouth gaped in wonder. "Please what? Please stop or please make me come?" he asked, his words breezing across her moist flesh.

The sounds of her harsh breathing filled the air as she looked down at him. "Make me come," she whispered. "Please."

Chance smiled like a wolf as he lowered his head and circled her bud with his tongue before flicking the tip against the smooth flesh with rapid speed meant to tease, to titillate, to arouse and to make his woman go crashing headfirst into an explosive orgasm. He had to lock his arms around her thighs to keep her in place as she wrestled between enjoying the pleasure and being driven mad by it.

And while she was deep in the throes of her cli-max, he rose from her just long enough to shed his clothes and sheathe himself. To be as naked as she. To relieve his aching erection. He hungered for her and could not wait one more moment to be inside her.

Chance thrust his hard inches inside her swiftly. Deeply.

Ngozi reached out blindly and gripped the wrought iron railing of her staircase, not caring about the hard edge of the step bearing into her lower back or how each of his wild thrusts caused her buttocks to be chafed by the wood.

Chance lifted up his upper body to look down at her as he worked his hips back and forth. Each stroke caused his hardness to slide against the moist ridges of her intimacy. She was lost. To time. To place. To reason.

"Here it comes," he whispered down to her.

She gasped as his inches got harder right as he quickened his thrusts and climaxed inside her, flinging his head back, the muscles of his body tensing as he went still and roughly cried out in pure pleasure.

Wrapping her ankles behind his strong thighs, Ngozi worked her hips in a downward motion that pulled on the length of him.

Chance swore.

Ngozi had a devilish little smile, taking over as she worked her walls and flexed her hips to send him over the edge into the same mindless pleasure he brought her. And when he gave a shriek similar to the falsetto of an opera singer and tried to back out of her, she locked him in place and continued to work every bit of his release from him.

"Please," he begged, wincing and biting his bottom lip.

"Please what? Huh? Please stop, or please make me come some more?" she asked, her tone flirtatiously mocking in between hot little pants of her own.

"*Please* stop," he pleaded.

She stopped her sex play, but with him still inside

her, she sat up and pulled his face down to kiss his mouth a dozen or more times. "Don't you ever forget that I love you, too," she whispered against his lips, searching his eyes and seeing that all her doubts of his feelings for her had been for naught.

The next weeks for Chance and Ngozi seemed to fly by. Happiness and being in love had a way of snatching time. And they were happy. Their time apart had brought on changes both needed to be able to love someone properly.

Life was good.

Ding-dong.

Ngozi was lounging on her sofa reading through briefs. She picked up her tablet and checked the security system, frowning at the sight of Chance's mother, Esmerelda, standing on her front doorstep.

Well, life was almost good.

She dropped the tablet and the back of her head onto the sofa as she released a heavy sigh. *What could she possibly want?*

Ngozi avoided Esmerelda at all costs. Although she and Chance had reconciled, they'd never discussed his mother or her clear dislike of her son's choice for love. "Hell, I'm not the one who left him at the altar," she muttered, rising from the sofa to pad barefoot out of the room and over to the front door.

Ding-dong.

Ngozi paused and frowned with an arched brow. "A'ight now," she warned.

She allowed herself one final inhale and exhale

of breath with a prayer for patience before opening the door with a smile that felt too wide and too false. "Hello, Ms. Diaz. How can I help you?" she said.

Esmerelda was a beautiful woman of just her late forties. Having had Chance at such a young age, she physically did not look that much older than him. She stood there in a strapless red dress with her hair in a messy topknot. Ngozi couldn't deny that she was beautiful.

"May I come in?" she asked, looking past Ngozi's shoulder.

"Chance isn't here," she immediately explained.

"Yes, I know," Esmerelda said. "He's at the offices for Second Chances."

Very true. Yes, he was. Of course, she would know that. Esmerelda and Chance were very close, Ngozi knew, but she also felt they were too close. *Hell, does she think anyone is good enough for him?*

"So, may I come in?" Esmerelda asked again.

Ngozi nodded and stepped back, pulling the door open along with her. "Right this way," she said, closing the door and leading her into the family room.

"That is a beautiful painting," Esmerelda said, moving to stand in front of the fireplace and look up at the artwork Ngozi had hung there the day of the Spring Bazaar.

Three svelte women in floral print dresses with large wide-brimmed hats that covered their faces sat in a field of flowers. "It is *The Gossiping Neighbors* by—"

"Juan Eduardo Martinez," Esmerelda provided,

turning to offer her a smile. "I am very familiar with his work."

"Chance introduced me to him and some other Dominican painters with the art he has at his house," Ngozi said, crossing her arms over her chest in the strapless woven cotton jumpsuit she wore.

"Yes, *I* introduce *him* to our culture any time we are back in Cabrera," she said with pride.

Ngozi nodded. "We flew there last weekend and it really is a beautiful city, Ms. Diaz," she said.

Esmerelda looked around at the room, taking in the vibrant colors and artwork. "Do you mean that or are you just saying it?" she asked.

"I mean it or I wouldn't have said it," Ngozi said, feeling offended.

Esmerelda looked surprised by Ngozi's push back. "I don't know," she said with a shrug and downturn of her ruby red lips as she dragged a finger across the edge of the wooden table.

The hell...

"Ms. Diaz, I love your son. I r*eally* do. I mean, I thought I would never be blessed with happiness after losing my husband. At first I didn't know what I did to deserve a second chance. I actually thought I didn't, but now I know I am just as good and decent and caring as he is. We are *good* for each other," Ngozi stressed. "And if you can't see that I make your son happy, then you just don't want him to be happy with me or maybe anybody else. I just really wished you had been this vigilant with Helena and saved him the heartache and shame."

Esmerelda's eyes lit up and she rubbed her fingers together, like she was excited by Ngozi's spunk and candor. "Hello, Ngozi Johns, it's nice to finally meet the *real* you," she said, extending her hand.

Ngozi looked down at it guardedly. "Huh?" she asked.

"I thought you were a phony blowhard like the Blonde Devil, and it's good to see a difference in you," she explained, her hand still offered. "I fed you the spiciest meal I have ever cooked, and you still swallowed it down to avoid angering Chance's mother. You wouldn't even speak up for yourself. I saw you as docile and weak. That is not the type of woman my son needs."

Ngozi was surprised at the woman's discernment. They'd met just once, and she saw right through the facade.

"I told him this and my Chance kept insisting that you were fiery, strong and had no problem telling him when he was wrong. I wanted to see this for myself and I didn't...until just now," Esmerelda said, actually offering Ngozi a smile. "I know my son. Sometimes, not all the time, but *sometimes* he needs to be challenged and pushed. Push him to be the best man he can be, and then my job can be done, Ngozi."

She nodded, feeling relief as she finally took Esmerelda's hand into her own. "I will because he does the same for me."

"Good," Esmerelda said, releasing her hand and turning to open her tote to remove a teal canister with delicate flowers. She handed it to Ngozi. "Recipes of my son's favorite Dominican dishes. Learn to feed him something besides sex. *Bueno?*"

Ngozi took the can and laughed. *"Si,"* she said, holding the canister to her chest.

Esmerelda reached for her purse and headed out of the room, pausing at the entrance. "The only two secrets I want you to keep from Chance are that you have those recipes and that I was here today," she said before turning and leaving.

Ngozi didn't have a chance to walk her to the door.

Instead, she opened the canister and sifted through the recipe cards. They were photocopies of the originals Esmerelda obviously wasn't ready to part with.

Feed him something besides sex.

Ngozi could only laugh.

Chance was watching television as they lounged in Ngozi's master suite, having decided to spend the night at her home in Passion Grove instead of at his in Alpine. He glanced over at where she had been reading Colson Whitehead's *Underground Railroad.* The book was lying on the lounge chair in front of the window, and she stared outside at the late summer night.

"Something wrong?" he asked.

Ngozi glanced over at him with a soft smile. "Today would have been my brother's birthday," she said.

Chance used the remote to turn the television off and then rolled off the bed in nothing but his sleep pants to walk over and straddle the lounge as he sat closely behind her. He pressed a kiss to her shoulder and then her nape. Finally, she had shared more with him about her brother's death and its impact on her family's life, just as he told her about meeting his father and discovering he had three half siblings—none of which he was prepared to deal with in the manner it called for. Ngozi had made sure he knew that she wanted him to reach out and meet his siblings sooner rather than later. It was clear her longing for her deceased brother intensified her feelings on his relationship, or lack thereof, with his siblings.

"If he was here, what would you give him for his birthday?" he asked, redirecting his thoughts back to her as he leaned to the side to watch her beautiful profile.

"Oh wow, I never thought about it," she said, looking reflective. "He used to love comic books, so I would've bought out a whole theater and watched *Black Panther* with him," she said, nodding. "He would've loved that movie."

"Or you could have just brought him over to my theater at the house," Chance reminded her, massaging her upper arms.

"True," she agreed. "Sometimes I forget you're a billionaire."

"And that's one of the reasons I want to marry you," he said, meaning to surprise her with his admission.

He felt her body go stiff before she turned on the lounge to face him.

"Chance," she said.

"Ngozi," he returned, digging into the pocket of his pants and removing the box he had placed there.

The plan had been to slip it under the pillows and propose after making love to her, but the moment seemed perfect.

"Whoo," she exclaimed as she caught sight of the large diamond solitaire atop a band of diamonds.

"Are you saying yes?" he asked, feeling so much love for her and no fear of laying his heart on the line once again.

"Are you *asking* me?" she said gently with a pointed look at the floor.

"Right," he agreed, chuckling as he rose from the seat to lower his body to one knee and take her hand in his.

"Marry me, Ngozi, and love me just the way I need you to, and I promise to love and to cherish you just as you need to be loved and cherished. I want nothing more than to create a family with you. To love and be tempted by you for the rest of my life," he said earnestly, hiding none of his love for her.

Ngozi nodded. "I will love you forever and always, Chance Castillo," she swore as he slid the hefty ring onto her finger.

"Mi tentacion," he whispered to her as he rose and pulled her body up against his and kissed her with enough love and passion to last a lifetime.

Epilogue

Three months later

Ngozi felt sexy as she came down the stairs of Chance's mansion in Alpine in the beautiful silver beaded sheath dress she'd seen in the window of Spree the very same day she reconciled with Chance. She had returned to the upscale boutique and purchased the dress the very next day. She now finally had just the right opportunity to wear it.

A celebration.

She looked over at Chance, looking ever so handsome in his black-on-black tuxedo as he awaited her. *Life is good.*

Chance's foundation, Second Chances, had just received a multimillion-dollar grant to help fund its philanthropic efforts toward underserved and sorely underrepresented lower-income defendants unable to afford bail or bond. With Ngozi's involvement as cochair of the board, the foundation's efforts would also expand to recruit skilled attorneys for pro bono work, including helping innocent men serving time for crimes they did not commit. Together, Chance and Ngozi were determined to effect change with the unfair treatment of people of color within the judicial system.

"Ready?" Ngozi called over to him, striking a pose.

Chance turned, and his eyes instantly went to the short hem lightly stroking her legs midthigh. "Worth the wait, Ngozi," he said, now looking at her face as he came over to her.

They shared a brief but passionate kiss.

When his hands rose to grip her buttocks, she reluctantly shook her head. "We have a whole party and all our family and friends waiting for us at Alek and Alessandra's," she reminded him, using her thumb to rub her crimson gloss from his lips.

"To *hell* with that party," he growled low in his throat.

"Don't you want to celebrate the sale of your second app, Mr. Tech King?" she teased.

He smiled, and it slowly broadened. "Tech King, huh?"

She shrugged one bare shoulder. "*Forbes*' words, not mine," she said, accepting his hand as they crossed the foyer together.

"Not bad for a kid from the projects?" Chance asked as he opened the front door for her.

She glanced up and stroked his cheek as he passed. "Not bad at all," she assured him.

The sun had disappeared, but the summer evening was still warm as they made their way to Chance's new white Lamborghini—a celebratory gift.

He deserves it.

She looked around at the beautiful grounds of his estate before climbing inside the car. "You sure you're not going to miss all this?" she asked him once he was behind the wheel in the driver's seat.

"We're building from scratch. I'll be fine," he assured her.

Ngozi covered his hand on the stick shift with her own. "Good, because I really want our home base to be in Passion Grove," she said as she eyed the ornate bronzed for-sale sign just outside his exterior gate.

She had gladly given up her rental. Its purpose in her newfound independence had been served.

Chance chuckled. "Can you believe I used to make fun of Alek for moving to a small town?" he asked, accelerating the sports car forward.

"Yes, but Passion Grove is no ordinary small town," she said, thinking of the ability to maintain its charms but still perfectly blend with luxury.

"Damn straight it's not."

Chance pulled the car to a smooth stop at a red light. His hand went to one of her exposed thighs.

She released a little grunt of pleasure. "I can't wait to let everyone in on our secret, Mr. Castillo," she said.

Chance smiled as he looked over at her. "Me either, Mrs. Castillo," he said.

Just that morning they had followed their impulses and flew to Vegas to get married. Neither longed for a huge event after their past experiences with such—his nuptials never happened and hers led to anything but marital bliss.

They chose to focus on their marriage and not the wedding.

"My *tentadora*," Chance said, indulging himself with a kiss.

"Will I always be your *temptress*?" she asked, her voice and her eyes soft with her love for him.

"Until death do us part."

"Now *that* sounds tempting."

* * * * *

Get 4 FREE REWARDS!

We'll send you 2 FREE Books plus 2 FREE Mystery Gifts.

Harlequin® Desire books feature heroes who have it all: wealth, status, incredible good looks... everything but the right woman.

FREE
Value Over
$20

YES! Please send me 2 FREE Harlequin® Desire novels and my 2 FREE gifts (gifts are worth about $10 retail). After receiving them, if I don't wish to receive any more books, I can return the shipping statement marked "cancel." If I don't cancel, I will receive 6 brand-new novels every month and be billed just $4.55 per book in the U.S. or $5.24 per book in Canada. That's a savings of at least 13% off the cover price! It's quite a bargain! Shipping and handling is just 50¢ per book in the U.S. and 75¢ per book in Canada*. I understand that accepting the 2 free books and gifts places me under no obligation to buy anything. I can always return a shipment and cancel at any time. The free books and gifts are mine to keep no matter what I decide.

225/326 HDN GMYU

Name (please print)

Address   Apt. #

City   State/Province   Zip/Postal Code

Mail to the **Reader Service:**
IN U.S.A.: P.O. Box 1341, Buffalo, NY 14240-8531
IN CANADA: P.O. Box 603, Fort Erie, Ontario L2A 5X3

Want to try two free books from another series? Call 1-800-873-8635 or visit www.ReaderService.com.

---

*Terms and prices subject to change without notice. Prices do not include applicable taxes. Sales tax applicable in N.Y. Canadian residents will be charged applicable taxes. Offer not valid in Quebec. This offer is limited to one order per household. Books received may not be as shown. Not valid for current subscribers to Harlequin Desire books. All orders subject to approval. Credit or debit balances in a customer's account(s) may be offset by any other outstanding balance owed by or to the customer. Please allow 4 to 6 weeks for delivery. Offer available while quantities last.

Your Privacy—The Reader Service is committed to protecting your privacy. Our Privacy Policy is available online at www.ReaderService.com or upon request from the Reader Service. We make a portion of our mailing list available to reputable third parties that offer products we believe may interest you. If you prefer that we not exchange your name with third parties, or if you wish to clarify or modify your communication preferences, please visit us at www.ReaderService.com/consumerschoice or write to us at Reader Service Preference Service, P.O. Box 9062, Buffalo, NY 14240-9062. Include your complete name and address.

826

810

4846.

Ysanne
HR Systems
Analyst

2.01
1.01

368

*

David
not
sensing
priorities.